EVEN THE PREACHER GOT A SIDE CHICK

By:

Angie Hayes

Even The Preacher Got A Side Chick

©Copyright 2016 Angie Hayes

Published by:

Cachet Presents

First Trade Paperback Edition Printing 2016

ISBN-13: 978-1530424856

ISBN-10: 1530424852

Dedication

This book is solely dedicated to my mother; Mrs. Joyce Thomas. Not only were you my father, the late great Reverend Robert Thomas first lady, but you're also mine. Love you ma!

THE LORD IS MY SHEPPARD AND I SHALL NOT WANT

FATIMA

Look at this mutha'fucka, standing up there in front of all these people lying his ass off! He's up there reciting the devotion as if I didn't catch his ass in some tramp pussy last night at a cheap ass motel! I guess this chick must not be important; considering the others ones I caught him with were at classier places.

I thought to myself as I watched Deacon Travis Whitehead; my lying, cheating, sorry, no-good ass husband stand in front of the church and act like he is a man of God. When in reality, he is nothing but Satan's distant cousin. People tend to think that it's the Pastor's wives that have it bad, but nobody ever stops to think about the deacons and the shit they have going on. You see, the Pastors are what you call the representation of the church; the teacher of the classroom.

Their name is what represents us, but in reality they have no actual power. Just like the President of the United

States. He can want things to happen and pass laws, but it has to be voted in by congress. That is what the deacons are of the church, congress. When it comes to choosing who to represent the church, fundraisers, the pastor salaries, hell even replacing the pastor, the deacons are the ones who make those decisions.

But the real HNIC is the head deacon, and that's my husband. He's in the background calling all the shots and fucking everything with a skirt on walking in the process. I've been married to Travis now for six long years; and let me tell you if I would have known then what I know now, I would have run the other way soon as he suggested we have coffee that day. I wish God would have sent his ass over to me with a neon caution warning sign flashing.

I had relocated to Alexandria, Ohio from Memphis, Tennessee and was an ER nurse. It was a big, yet sudden move from me. I had just come out of a seven year relationship with my first love Evan, after I caught him fucking my best friend. That broke me so bad that I knew I couldn't continue to live in the same zip code as those two, so I put in an application in a small town hospital with hopes of getting hired quick. Soon as I was called in for an interview not knowing if I would get hired or not, I packed all clothes, shoes and personal belongings and made that 9 ½ hour drive. I admit I was running away from all the hurt and embarrassment back at home. But I wasn't strong enough to deal with it all back then.

I ended up getting hired on the spot. That was the one of the perks of working in a small populated town; they didn't need time to make decisions. Your first impression is all they really needed. I had a nice piece of change in my checking and savings account, so within a week I was fully employed and renting out a nice, cozy two bedroom apartment. I fell right into the routine of my new life as if nothing in my past existed.

The only people I ever talked to back home were my parents. I was the only child and have always been close to them. All of my friends (including my trifling ass ex and slimy best friend) were cut completely off by me. I just couldn't deal with the questions from them or the tired excuses as to why shit happened. I just wanted to start over and go where no one knew me or my story.

It was a Friday night and the ER was relatively slow. I wasn't use to it being a slow day at work like this at a hospital especially on weekends, but I welcomed the calm. I was sitting at my desk updating some charts into my computer when my co-worker, Tonya handed me an ER chart of a patient that had just come in.

"Finally you have some action tonight Fatima, just not the action you need!" Tonya said laughing as she handed me the chart.

Tonya and I had become real cool with one another since I started working here. It was a relief to have at least one girlfriend to talk to and occasionally hang with in a new place.

"Trust me, I don't need that action." I said shaking my head as I took the chart from her hand.

"Well honey, that there in that room waiting to be seen by you is a fine piece of well-seasoned meat, have fun!" Tonya said as she left my station.

I walked down the hall towards the room shaking my head and laughing at her remarks. I knocked on the door twice before entering the room.

"Hello Mr. Whitehead, I'm Nurse Reed and I will be taking a look at you today" I said as I looked up from the chart and noticed this indeed fine specimen sitting up on the table.

I had to make sure I didn't stare and remain professional.

"Hello Nurse Reed. It's nice to meet a beautiful woman like you." he said to me flashing a nice smile with perfectly white teeth.

"Thank you for the compliment, it says here that you have been having chest pains is that correct?"

"Yes ma'am. It's been going on now for the past two days."

"Two days, well can you unbutton your shirt and let's what's going on." I said as I pulled my stethoscope from around my neck and put them on my ears.

As he took his shirt off, I noticed how incredibly fit he was. I pressed the diaphragm on his bare chest and asked him to breath in an and out slowly so I could hear his breathing. I noticed how muscular his chest was as if he lived in the gym. Once I asked him to breathe again, I told him he could put his shirt back on and took a seat on the stool in front of him. As I notated his chart, I felt his eyes on me.

"So Mr. Whitehead, do you have any stress going on in your life right now?" I asked probing trying to see what is causing his chest pains.

"No. I'm living stress-free." He replied smiling again.

"Ok good, how are your eating habits?"

"My eating habits are fairly healthy, with the exception of a good home-cooked southern Sunday dinner every Sunday, but I make sure I work it off come Monday morning in the gym." He replied.

I can damn sure see that!" I thought to myself.

As I was noting everything down, I noticed on his chart that he was 41 years old; seventeen years my senior. He surely didn't look it though.

"Ok Mr. Whitehead, I'm gonna have you take an EKG, chest x-ray and a CT scan test. I just want to make sure that nothing serious is going on with you. Another nurse will be right in to take you to get your tests done and I will see you afterwards with the doctor to go over the results with you" I said as I got up to leave.

For some reason, I had to hurry up and rush out of the room before he noticed that I was starting to get uncomfortable. I don't know what it was about this man, hell I didn't even know him. He was just a patient of mine. After about an hour and a half, I met back up with him again accompanying the doctor with his test results.

"Well Mr. Whitehead, it looks like you just have a bad case of heartburn. Some antacids and less of those fattening Sunday dinners will cure this right on up. I'll have Nurse Reed write you up a prescription of antacids. If you have and more problems, please don't hesitate to come back and see me" the doctor said as he stood up and left the room, leaving us there alone again.

"Now ain't this something funny. All this time it was nothing but gas." Travis said laughing up a storm.

"Don't feel bad, we get this all the time. It's very easy to mistake gas or heartburn with something more serious like a heart attack." I said as I handed him his prescription and discharged papers.

"Say Ms. Reed. I know this might be out of line but I would love to take you for a cup of coffee and get to know you better, especially since you're new around here."

"How do you know I'm new here?" I questioned with a raised eyebrow.

"Well this is a small town and I know just about everybody here, so when a new face comes along I can point it out."

At that point, I couldn't contain my blushing. I haven't had male attention like this since Evan. I know I should have kept it professional and declined his invitation, but I just couldn't resist. His charm and the fact that he was older than me made me curious to see what he was about. Never the less, we exchanged numbers that night and agreed to meet up for coffee the following morning.

Over coffee, I learned that not only was Travis 41 which was twelve years my senior; he had a twenty three year old daughter from a previous marriage, and was also a Deacon at New Faith Missionary Baptist Church. All of this was new to me. Not only have I never had someone

7

interested in me that was way older than me, but to be a deacon at that. After our first *date* as I considered it, it was Fatima and Travis since then.

This man whined me, dined me and fucked me every which way sideways! Before Travis all I knew was Evan, so to be exposed to all these new things by someone much older was very inviting. After about six months of us dating, Travis popped the question and of course I accepted with no hesitation with the diamond cut 11 carat ring placed on my finger. We ended up having a small intimate wedding here in Alexandria with just my parents attending from my side. They weren't exactly thrilled about me marrying a man they never met prior to us getting married, let alone a much older man; but my parents expressed that if I was happy, so were they.

Now here it is six years later and I was more miserable than ever! It seemed like once we said I do, Travis peeled off the façade and showed his true trifling ass colors! I found out that I was not his second wife like I had first thought, but I was in fact his third! Then the women started coming out the woodworks with constantly letting me know they were fucking my husband, calling my phone and even coming up to the church to try and let their presence be known. In the beginning I just turned a blind eye to everything.

I honestly had it embedded in my mind, along with Travis convincing me that these women were just jealous of us. Here he was a man with a high reputation as being the head Deacon in the town's church, good looking and very successful with his own construction company. He married me, this young, fine new comer in town and folks were jealous. But as the years went on, the women kept coming and the lies kept piling. Travis started getting comfortable with the fact that he had this young wife who gave up her passion of being a nurse and settled on being a dutiful wife.

Then he got sloppy or just stop giving a damn all together. The constant coming home late, the hickeys on his neck, the unexpected money that would be missing out of our checking account, and whatever woman he was dealing with at that time would always try to make it known, especially to me. I was taking the disrespect so much in the beginning until I became numb to it. But now I'm getting sick and tired of this shit. That's right. After six years, I'm finally tired of Travis and this bullshit ass marriage, along with this church.

Last night the mutha'fucka acted like he didn't know where his home was when I had been calling him all day, so I took it upon myself to call OnStar to track his Escalade and it led me right to the Super 8 motel where he was at with some tramp. I banged on the door and when she opened it naked; I dragged that hoe out by her hair and beat her ass down in the parking lot. This wasn't my first go round giving out ass whooping's over Travis, but this time it was different. I wasn't beating her ass over him; I was taking my years of anger and frustration out on her. At that point, I could have given a fuck about who Travis was fucking, but I was tired of him continuing to do it like I was just invisible.

When Travis finally pulled me off of his latest jump-off, I hauled back and slapped his ass in the eye as hard as I could. As he bent over in pain, I made my way back to my brand new Mercedes S550 and hauled ass back home. That night I was sleeping peacefully in bed when I heard Travis finally bring his ass home. Once he finished his business in the bathroom, he got into bed on his side and I assumed drifted off to sleep. Although I was turned over on my side and acted like I didn't have a care in the world, I was crying my silent tears. All of this was becoming a routine for me and I hated it.

After Travis was finished with devotion, he lifted his head up and wiped the sweat from his brow. I saw that he winced in pain as he rubbed against his eye with the handkerchief. He had already told folks earlier when we got to church that he hit it on the closet door this morning when opening it. I sat there smirking as I watched him gently try to dab the sweat off his bruised eye. Little did he know, that if he kept fucking with me he was gone be in a lot more pain than that.

TRAVIS

I swear if I could get away with it, I would strangle the shit out of Fatima's ass for hitting me in my eye like that. If she hadn't pulled off from the parking lot, I think I might have. I know I was wrong for messing around on my wife, but it was just in my nature. I've always been a ladies man. Growing up, my daddy used to take me with him when he went to go visit his women and schooled me on life.

He also made me promise to never tell my momma because if I did she would take me away from him, so I never mentioned a word. Even when we would come back from seeing a woman friend of his and my momma would accuse him, I still wouldn't say anything. I loved my daddy and I loved my momma. But my daddy and I had a special bond. Everything my daddy taught me and every word he said to me, I made sure to listen.

When he told me that a man wasn't put on this earth to have just one woman, but to have just that one woman to keep his home right, I believed him. I watched my daddy go to work every day and bust his ass and come home and give my momma his check to pay the bills. We never wanted for anything and lived quit comfortable, especially for an African American family back then. So I saw nothing wrong with him going out from time to time and having a little fun. I always thought my momma was just nagging my daddy and needed to be more grateful.

Daddy told me under no circumstances that he would leave my momma for any woman out here, and he never did until he passed away back in 2000 of liver cancer. By that time, I was with my second wife Loretta. I got married to my first wife straight out of high school thinking I was in love and wanted a wife at home like my momma, but after a year of that she realized she didn't want to be married so she up and left and sent me back some divorce papers. Shortly after that, I met Patrice who told me she wanted nothing more than to be a wife and mother, so I married her. She got pregnant and had our daughter Regan. Six years into the marriage, Patrice was diagnosed with ovarian cancer and since the doctor didn't catch it in time, it took her rather quickly.

After her passing, it was just me and my baby girl who was five at the time. With the exception of my momma helping me out with her, I was all she had. I had made it up in my mind then that I didn't want to remarry and decided to give myself to the Lord. That's when I joined New Faith Missionary Baptist Church, and have been here ever since. I was shocked when the pastor came up to me one night after bible study and asked me if I would like to be nominated to the deacon board.

Even though I was a faithful and heavy tithe payer, I knew it had something to do with the fact that, prior to the evening; I had walked in on him and his secretary fucking in his office. I just apologized and quickly closed his door. I'm a firm believer on what a man does with another woman is his business and this was no exception. So when Pastor Evans approached me with the offer, I gladly accepted. That following week I was voted in by the rest of the church board members and man has my life been a rollercoaster ever since!

I thought the pastor was the one that got major pussy in the church, but the deacons got our fair share! Once the pastor announced that I was now a deacon in front of the congregation that Sunday, women started lining up for a piece of this good dick! I mean I wasn't a bad looking man. I was 6'3 with a nice muscular build and smooth chocolate skin. I always kept a neat low boy haircut with waves for days and a matching goatee.

I never had a problem getting women, but being a

deacon now made it to where I didn't have to do anything, it all came to me. I enjoyed all the attention I was getting from the women and as much pussy as I wanted. Hell me and Pastor Evans both! We tag teamed these women so much that after about three months of being on the deacon board, he suggested that I be moved up to be head deacon! Even though there were questions as to how he could suggest that in such a short period of time for someone like me who had just got on, it got pushed through and I was accepted.

It was then that I was told by the church board that I needed to settle down and find a wife, that it would be a good look for the church as well. It was just by faith that night I went to the Emergency room for chest pains that I met Fatima. I knew she was new in town, because I would have noticed her sexy ass and beautiful face beforehand. The fact this she was younger than me was a bonus as well.

She was twelve years my junior and I knew that I could mold her into being the woman and wife of the church deacon that I needed her to be. I admit, I ended up falling in love with her in the process; but I easily got bored as well. You see, Fatima was home; my safety net. When I was done with who I was dealing with in the streets, I knew I had a woman and a home to come to. That's the way my daddy did it and it seemed to work out fine for him.

In the beginning of our marriage, Fatima went with the flow. Didn't question me about shit and just catered to me like she should, like the bible said she has too! But as the years started going by, her ass became a fucking nag. Wanting to know where I was at or who was calling my phone. Then questioning why money was missing out of our account.

I had to remind her ass that ever since we said 'I Do', she didn't have to lift a finger to work. I made sure she stayed in the latest clothes, diamonds dripping from which ever body part she wanted, newest car off the show room floor and house where she could lay her whole fucking family head and still have plenty room left over! So whatever else I chose to spend my fucking money on was none of her damn business!

I assume my infidelities started taking its toll on her because she started acting out! Hell every other woman I fucked with, Fatima somehow found out and whooped they asses. But that shit didn't matter to me, because once my wife found out about one, I moved on to the next. Alexandria may be small, but I carried much weight around here and could get anything I set my hands on and dick in.

PAUL

"That's right bitch, suck this dick like yo' life depends on it!" I grunted as Candice was down between my legs sucking my dick as if she was trying to clear the skin off this muthafucka!

"Hmm you like this shit daddy?" she asked as she came up for air while licking on the head.

"You know I do, now put that shit back in ya mouth so I can bless that throat." I demanded as I gripped the back of her ponytail and shoved my piece down her throat.

With the feeling of her warm breath and suctioning tongue around the grasp of my dick again, within minutes I exploded down her throat. She knew the routine to stay down there and suck every last drop until I was done. Money and good sperm were the two things I damn sure hated to waste.

"Whew! Girl you damn sure know how to make sure I start my day off right" I said catching my breath as Candice stood up licking her tongue across her top lip.

"You know I have to take care of my man. I definitely don't know want any other bitch doing it." She replied as she went into the bathroom in my office.

Seconds later I heard the water running. She came back into the room with a warm cloth and proceeded to wash my dick off thoroughly. Once she was done, she licked the head once more and tucked it back into my briefs before walking back off to the bathroom. I was still leaning on the front of my desk trying to catch my composure from that heavy ass nut I just released.

"So what do you have planned today?" Candice asked coming back into the room fixing herself.

"I have a couple of meetings and then I'm having lunch with your father to see where we are with the ideas for the new church." I explained as I fixed my belt buckle.

"Well while y'all talking, maybe you can try and convince him to ease up on his bank account and stop being so damn stingy! I know it's that fucking bitch ass wife of his though. Ever since he married Fatima, things between him and I haven't been the same." Candice complained.

Every time I mentioned her father, she would always bring up how he's not giving her money like he use too and blaming it on his wife. But the truth was, he got tired of always having to pay thousands of dollars to American

Express every month because Candice was too fucking lazy to get a job and support her 'wanna be living like the Joneses' habits.

If you haven't figured it out by now, I'm Reverend Paul Stanley; Pastor of New Faith Missionary Baptist church, and I just had my friend, head of my deacon board, Travis' daughter sucking my dick like Jesus was about to come back down and give her a reward for a job well done! Ever since Candice turned 18, I've been fucking that pussy, mouth and ass with no remorse. I was the first she ever had and if I had my say, I'll be her last. But I knew that wasn't gone happen. Candice was a nice piece of young ass I enjoyed, but I also knew if a man came along with more money and power than me, then she'll be strapped on his dick next.

I know what y'all thinking: He's a preacher! Now don't get me wrong, I love the Lord and I knew I had a calling to preach his word since the age of 12 which is why I tried to live by his word and attend Seminary School after I graduated High School. I didn't smoke, drink, curse or fornicate. My goal in life was to learn and understand the word of God and teach it to those who didn't understand it. And also make sure I fall in love and marry the woman God created for me to be by my side.

One I finished seminary school; I set out to do just

those things. I met my wife Karla when I went to visit a church in North Carolina. She was the most beautiful woman I had ever laid eyes on! She had a petite build with ass and titties that fit her frame just right. Her hair had a natural curly texture to it that just flowed a little past her shoulders and bounced freely. She was creole mixed so her complexion was smooth.

She had light brown eyes and a beautiful smile that displayed dimples. When I was in the pulpit that Sunday as the guest pastor, it was hard for me to concentrate on what I was teaching because I was so distracted by her. Once I was done, imagine my surprise when the pastor of that church introduced me to his family and I learned that she was his daughter! I knew right then and there that she was the one I was gonna marry and have by my side to lead my flock.

Twelve years later, I'm the pastor of my own church and still married to the woman I fell in love with from the first time I laid eyes on her. But hear me when I say this, neither of us are the same people we were back then! With becoming the head of my own church came power, money and all of the unlimited pussy that I could ever want! When Karla and I first got married, it was her idea to start our own ministry in a small town and build our way up and that's exactly what we did! Since we came to Alexandria our lives haven't been the same.

My wife, who was once a quiet, church going young lady, became a fashionista first lady. She wore nothing but the best, had personal shoppers, drove cars that had to be imported, she never wore the same suit and hat to church twice, and whenever she stepped out on the scene, everyone knew who she was. My wife carried herself with so much swag and grace that she was on a pedestal all her own. But just like the power, money and pussy went to my head; the spotlight of being the first lady went to hers as well.

Gradually through time, she stopped doing the things a wife is supposed to do. I stopped getting those good home cooked meals from her, and started eating what our cook that she hired cooked. She stopped picking out my suits for Sunday Services and left that up to our maid to handle. She stop fucking me four to five times a week like we use too, and now I'd be lucky if she gave me the ass once a month! All Karla cares about is her appearance and making sure I stay on top of my game so her ass can stay up top with me!

Somewhere along the way, I let all the things I was against take over my life and now I can't seem to get shit back under control. Hell in all honesty, I don't even know if I want shit to change!

"Did you hear me Paul?" Candice asked standing in

front of me breaking me out of my thoughts.

"Look baby girl, I told you before that I can't discuss you with yo' daddy. That'll make things look suspicious. Especially with me asking him to give you more money to support your shopping habits. You graduated from college so why don't you put your degree to use." I hinted to get her ass a job.

"Oh you want me to put my degree to use and get a job, but yet you got yo' stuck up ass wife living like she's Michelle Obama and not lifting a finger? Shit I'm fucking you too so why can I not sit on my ass and get paid for this pussy also?" Candice said a little louder than I wanted her to.

"First off, lower your damn voice while talking to me in my office! And I told you about worrying about what Karla got going on. She's the first lady and my wife and ain't shit changing that but God himself." I reminded her ass.

"Whatever Paul. Every time I mention your precious little wife you cop an attitude. I tell you what, maybe I should start looking elsewhere for somebody else who appreciates a good woman with good pussy, because it's obvious you don't appreciate this." Candice said lifting up her dress and revealing her juicy pussy with no panties on underneath.

My dick started jumping once I saw that pretty cat looking back at me. I had to quickly remind myself that I had somewhere to be, but I knew I most definitely had to take care of that later.

"Look do whatever it is you feel you need to do, but I gotta run. You know the routine, leave out quietly. When I'm done handling my business I'll call you so I can handle that there" I said pointing down to her pussy.

She just snatched her dress down roughly, grabbed her purse and walked out my office slamming the door. I shook my head as I gathered my things and left as well.

"Everything ok Pastor?" My secretary Shirley asked as I passed her desk.

"Everything is fine Shirley. I'll be gone for the rest of the day so only call me with the important calls and take messages for the rest. Have a blessed day" I said as I smiled heading to my car.

I knew Candice was pissed at me by the way she left, but she'll be ok. Once I'm done with meeting with her daddy, I'll make sure to punish that pussy.

KARLA

"I hate when you have to just leave so suddenly" I pouted as I rolled over and watched him put on his pants.

I had just finished getting my brains fucked out and wanted nothing more than to cuddle and lay on his chest, but as always the church came first.

"I know baby, but I gotta meet your husband for lunch. We need to go over the budget and he wants to see the designs I have for the new church. So you know its business first and pleasure later." Travis said as he walked over to the bed and kissed me passionately.

I loved this man and the way he made my body feel! If this was a perfect world I would be married to Travis instead of Paul's cheating lying ass, and would be happy. I know that I'm cheating also by sleeping with Travis, but I didn't start fucking around with Travis until I got tired of Paul and his whores.

When I first heard Paul preach at my father's church,

I knew he would be a man of power in the pulpit. The way he spoke he demanded your attention and the way he looked he wanted to be seen. He also knew he could preach! Growing up as a preacher's kid, I knew the difference between a pastor just show boating and yelling in the pulpit versus a pastor that really catches the spirit and that's exactly how Paul was.

Not to mention he was extremely sexy with his caramel skin, dark bedroom eyes, a sharp goatee with a clean shaven head. He reminded me so much of the actor Rockmond Dunbar from the series Soul Food. I was a virgin when we first met, but I had to ask God for forgiveness for the thoughts I was having while watching him preach his word. Surprised he asked me out once my father introduced us, things took off from there and less than a year later we were married.

I knew the kind of Pastor Paul could become given the right opportunity, so when I suggested that we start from the ground up on building a congregation in a small town, he jumped on the idea and we headed to Ohio. Once we got here, Paul said the spirit spoke to him and said we needed to settle in Alexandria and we've been here ever since.

I regret like hell I even suggested to my husband that he start pastoring in a small town because he hasn't been the same since! Don't get me wrong, I knew what baggage came along with becoming the first lady. I mean, I did see how my mother handled things growing up. She always had to take a backseat to the church, and I was prepared for that. But what I wasn't prepared for was taking a back seat and dealing with the lies, cheating, STD's and just blatant disrespect by my husband!

In the beginning, I tried to still be the submissive wife the bible said I should be. I ignored the late night so called meetings, coming home in the morning, the smell of perfume that lingered on his body that I knew I didn't wear, the nasty looks I would get from the other women at church or the hickeys on his chest.

But overtime, it all began to be too much. I wasn't dumb nor blind. I knew Paul was fucking around; and no matter how much I fucked my husband, be available whenever he needed me, made sure he had home cooked meals seven days a week, bills paid and take care of the house, his ass was still gone fuck around with other bitches.

So I decided to begin to do me and make myself become not only the baddest first lady these heffas laid eyes on, but also to also make sure Paul wouldn't continue to make a fool out of me.

That's why I switched shit up and stop doing the things I was once doing. I wanted Paul to know that I was far from the naive twenty-two year old he met in the beginning. Since he felt the need to go out there and still fuck around with these bum bitches after I gave him everything, I decided to let him have a go at it. But make no mistake about it; I wasn't worried about no bitch trying to take my spot! No matter how much pussy they threw at him or how hard they sucked on his dick, his ass knew he wasn't going anywhere!

"Believe me babe, I know how it goes. I know the church comes first" I said as I rolled over out of the bed and headed into the bathroom to freshen back up.

I cut the shower on and stepped inside. I grabbed my loofa and peach scented wash gel and began to try and wash the sin I constantly keep committing away. Travis has had this condo for about two years now without his wife Fatima's knowledge. Fatima. If that bitch only knew what she had in a man like Travis. She thought just because she was young that she could keep a tight hold on him, but her young ass didn't know how to tame a man like him. That's where I came in at. I finished washing up and rinsed off as I stepped back into the room wrapped in my towel hoping for a quickie before Travis left only to find him gone already. I saw that he left a note on the pillow.

Baby, I had to run but I promise you I'll make up for having to leave so soon. I'll call you later. Love, T

I smiled as I read the letter and began to get dressed. You damn right his ass is gonna make it up to me and he knows exactly how.

FATIMA

"Girl you did what?"

"You heard me. I said I grabbed that bitch by her hair and dragged her ass in the parking lot and tapped that ass!" I answered Tonya laughing.

We were having our monthly brunch and I was filling her in on the latest drama with Travis.

"I wish like hell I was there! I would have loved to see you paint the concrete with that trick. And what did Mr. Lover-Man do?"

"Girl he called himself trying to stop me from beating his hoe ass, but I knocked that nigga in his eye, jumped in my car and went home to sleep like a baby."

"Honey I don't know how you do it! That damn Travis would have caused me to catch plenty of cases and the serious one would be murder once I got done with his ass!" Tonya said as she took a sip from her margarita she was drinking.

Ever since I met her at the hospital that I use to work at before I married Travis, we have become the best of friends. Tonya was my girl and the one that pushed me into giving Travis a shot, but I won't hold that against her though. She can be the life of the party and also the one that will pop off at any time!

"Believe me when I say that I was close plenty of times to catching a murder charge behind his ass. But God is keeping me honey. I'm just so tired T." I sighed as I took a sip of my drink looking out into the water from our deck view.

"Uh um girl, you not tired." Tonya blurted out as she stopped drinking her drink.

"Yes I am." I assured her hoping I sound convincing.

"No you're not boo, because if you were yo ass wouldn't still be putting up with Travis and his doggish ways. You would be out here, living your life and fucking the world up alongside with me" Tonya said laughing.

I could tell she was trying to lighten the mood and make me laugh, and her crazy ass was doing just that.

"It's not that easy Tonya. Travis is my husband and I want to be able to say I gave my marriage my all before I throw in the towel. Besides, that wouldn't be a good look for the church. With Travis being the head deacon, him getting a divorce could tarnish that."

"Listen to me Fatima. You have given this marriage and that man your all, only to keep being disrespected, lied and cheated on! What more do you have to give? Shit, his ass is liable to come home with some type of nasty ass disease from one of these heffas and pass that shit to you, and it could be something shot and pills can't cure. You're a nurse, you know how that goes. As far as the church, I told you from the first time I visited there that it was a damn cult! Fuck Travis, fuck that church! You need to look out for you!" Tonya said a mouth full, and then she sat back in her chair and started back drinking her drink.

Before I could respond, I heard a familiar voice.

"Hey Fatima!" I turned around to see Karla walking up to our table.

"This bitch" I heard Tonya suck her teeth.

"Be nice." I said smiling through clenched teeth.

"Hey Karla, what are doing this way?" I asked her as we gave each other air kisses when she walked up to our table.

"I was heading over to the boutique. Marcus had some pieces flown in from New York and asked me to come in to see which pieces I wanted." Karla gloated.

I swear she thought she was damn Queen of

Alexandria with the way she acted. She felt that no one could out dress her or upstage her in anyway. This bitch even used the most openly gay dude around Alexandria to be her fucking flunky. Marcus portrayed to be her stylist but we all knew he wasn't anything but a yes man to her.

"That sounds like fun, maybe you should hurry up over there before they close" Tonya interrupted throwing major shade.

"Oh don't worry about me boo, they stay open for me no matter what so I'm good." Karla threw back at Tonya.

"Ok well it was good seeing you Karla, we were just about to leave so I'll catch up with you after church Sunday" I intervened so nothing would pop off.

"No problem. See you Sunday Fatima. Oh be sure to invite guests if you please, it's a lot of people in the world that needs Jesus" Karla sneered looking at Tonya as she put her shades back on and walked off.

"I promise you, that toothpick looking bitch got one more time to come for me and I swear she's the one that's gonna need Jesus when I'm done with her ass" Tonya said worked up.

Ever since I introduced Tonya and Karla to one another when Tonya first visited the church, she never cared too much for her. She said it was something about Kayla that rubbed her the wrong way and she just couldn't be trusted.

"Girl, come on and let's hit the mall so you can work off some of this extra estrogen you got going on" I said laughing as I got up and grabbed her arm to go.

I left money on the table since it was my turn to pay and we left to go do some damage to Travis' black card. Every time I catch his ass doing dirt, after I fuck them up, I make sure to put a dent in his wallet as well.

TRAVIS

"So I think we should narrow it down to these two designs here and have the committee vote on them ASAP so we can start building" I said to Paul as we sat in the back of the restaurant and looked over the layouts for the new church.

"Yea we do, they both look great but which one is the cheapest?" he asked laughing.

Although he seemed to be joking, I knew the less we spent on building the new church, the more money his ass could pocket. I knew the lifestyle and expenses Paula and Karla had, and it damn sure wasn't just from his salary the church was paying him. When I first was appointed head deacon, since I already had my own construction business, it was also suggested that I become over the trustee board as well.

They are the ones that handle the finances of the church, and since I was a business man, I was fit for the job.

That's when I started noticing that money was being skimmed off the top. The tithe amount that was marked on the envelope from tithe payers we recorded differently in the books. I also noticed that when collections were made or donations given for the Pastor's anniversary, none of the money went into the church funds like some of it should, but in fact all the money was gifted to the pastor!

Finally one night after bible study, I confronted Paul about my findings and that's when he offered to double my salary without the church knowing it. Now, money was never my issue and I damn sure wasn't short on it, but it was the idea of having more power than Paul once again. So I took the offer and continued to turn the blind eye of him robbing the church blind. His ass may think since he's the pastor that he's in control, but the truth is I'm the one that's in control!

I know his secrets, fucking his wife and getting paid extra so how I see it his ass is my bitch just as well as the other ladies I fuck with.

"Drawing B is the cheapest, if this is the route you wanna go I'll present it in front of the committee and let them know this design is the best and more efficient." I explained.

"Good! See that's why you're my right hand Travis. God knew what he was doing when he spoke to me and told me to appoint you as my best soldier."

Yeah right! I caught ya ass in some pussy other than Karla, that's why you appointed me to this position. God ain't have shit to do with this nigga! I thought to myself as I smirked at him.

"So now that we got the business part out of the way, you ready to tell me how you really got that damn black eye because I know it wasn't from no closet door" Paul asked smirking.

"Man Fatima caught my ass down at the Moe with Sister Patterson granddaughter and beat her ass. When I tried to stop it, she turned around and snuck my ass too in the eye" I reminisced shaking my head as I touched my eye.

"Oh you were there with freak ass Ebony. Yea, I had a piece of that too! You know she like it in the ass though." Travis said laughing.

"Yeah. I'm just glad Fatima didn't recognize her when she saw her; because I know she would have put on a show at church last Sunday."

"That she would have. Fatima is a young firecracker that's crazy about yo ass. Karla use to be the same way with me" Paul chuckled.

"Use to be, what happened?" I asked as if I didn't already know the answer.

"This life is what happened. Once I got in the

ministry, I let the devil use me more ways than he could. I love teaching the word, but no matter how much I pray to fight off the temptation of the skin, it always seems like the man wins first. I love Karla, she was sent by God to be my rib. And believe me when I say she put up with so much of my stuff that I still don't honestly know how she stayed around this long. I just believe that over the years, my antics have started to wear her down. I pay attention to my wife and I know she's tired. She stopped doing the things she used to do, that a wife is supposed to do. Now all she seems to care about is looking good and having the outside world thinking we're the damn perfect couple" Paul claimed.

"So you don't think she probably seeing somebody else?" I asked trying to see what it was he was actually thinking.

"Hell no! I mean she can't find no better than this here!" Paul leaned back in his chair displaying himself. "Besides, I'm still tearing that ass up damn near every night so she wouldn't even think about letting another nigga hit it. Her ass may be slack when it came to the kitchen, but she made up for it in the bedroom" Paul said smirking like a school boy.

I instantly became flustered and pissed. Karla swore me up and down that her and Paul weren't even sleeping in the same bedroom anymore let alone fucking! But yet I got this arrogant muthafucka sitting across from me bragging how he still fucking her ass!

"Aye man I hear that. But look, I need to wrap this up. I need to go home and make peace with the Mrs. I'll talk to you later, make sure you give Karla my love" I said cutting the lunch short as I got up to leave dapping Paul.

"No problem. And make sure you run that particular design by the board" He reminded me.

I nodded my head in approval, left my money for my portion of my bill on the table and left out. Soon as I got in my truck, I saw that I had a text message from Karla with a pic showing me shaven pussy with the message *she misses you already daddy.* I just laughed and deleted the message without responding. Shit from what I just heard, her pussy was getting plenty of attention and it just wasn't from me, I decided to head home to my wife and try to make up once again from the shit I've done.

FATIMA

Although Tonya and I had plans to go to the mall after brunch, she got called into the hospital for work so we had to take a rain check and I just headed on home. I missed working as a nurse and feeling that nurturing feeling of helping others. Once Travis and I were married, he didn't want me to work. He wanted me to stay at home and concentrate on being his wife and the future mother of his kids.

Kids was something I longed for in the beginning, but now I knew I couldn't bring a child into this world and fucked up situation of a marriage I'm in. That's why I take my birth control faithfully! A lot of women think a baby will fix their relationship, but I knew better than that!

Lord knows how many countless times I've been on bended knees asking him to fix my marriage and yet I'm still stuck dealing with the same disrespectful ass man! I'm trying hard to hold on, hoping Travis would finally get it and understand that I'm his wife and honor our vows better, but I'm losing hope. I pulled into our driveway, relieved to see that Travis truck wasn't in there meaning he wasn't home.

Every time I caught doing dirt, his ass would avoid me much as possible. Then he would come around with gifts and bullshit apologies as if it was supposed to make up for his dick being in another woman other than his wife. I grabbed the mail out the box and made my way inside the house. As I looked through the mail, I noticed it was nothing but bills so I sat them down on the entry way table in the foyer and went into the kitchen to grab me a bottle of water.

Soon as I grabbed my water, my doorbell rang. I wasn't expecting anybody, so I was curious as to who was at my door. I looked through the peephole to find Travis rude ass daughter Candice standing on my porch. The little bitch has the nerve to be standing out there like she had an attitude, tapping her feet waiting for me to answer the door. I was tempted to leave her ass standing out there, but I decided to just go ahead and see what it was she wanted so she can get her ass away from my house.

"What's up Candice." I answered the door less enthused.

"Well hello to you too Fatima, is my daddy here?" She asked walking up in my shit uninvited.

"Nope." I answered short as I closed the door.

"Do you know when he'll be back, I need to talk to him about something important." She stated sucking her teeth.

Take deep breathes Fatima because I know you're liable to fuck this little girl up!" I slowly said to myself before responding to her.

"I'm sorry Candice, I don't know what time your father will be home. Maybe you should try calling him and see." I suggested. I was trying my best to be civil to her ass, but over the years she had grown into this smart lil bitch who thought it was ok to keep trying me just because I was her step mother.

"Uh don't you think I did that already? If he would have answered his phone then I wouldn't be over here asking you!" she said getting slick out the mouth.

"Well I don't know what to tell you, other than the fact that he ain't here. Look, I just got in and I'm about to take a shower; so try coming back later when yo daddy here." I said as I went to open the door, holding it open for her ass to go.

The last thing I wanted to put up with right now was Candice and her brat ass attitude. I already knew she wanted to talk to her daddy about why she was suddenly limited on her spending; and I also knew she guessed I had something to do with it, which I did.

"Whatever Fatima. My daddy's probably with his other bitch anyway." She smirked in my face while passing by me heading out the door.

"That's fine. Maybe you should ask his other bitch to sponsor ya ass then. I know that's why you over here to talk to Travis, because your allowance has been cut short!" I laughed in her face. "Well let me confirm what I'm sure you already know, I told your daddy that it was time for yo ass to get a job! I don't give a damn who you are, but I refuse to sit back and let you keep racking up on bills that we have to pay!"

"We? Bitch that's my daddy's money and what he gives me has nothing to do with you!" Candice yelled out.

See, this is why I don't deal with this bitch! Because just like her daddy, she would cause me to catch a case!

"If that was the case, I wouldn't have a say so! And I said get a fucking job! Now bye, call ya daddy and if he with this *new bitch* then leave a message on his voice mail and I'm sure he'll call you back!" with that being said, I slammed the door in her fucking face and went upstairs to take a nice long, hot bath.

CANDICE

"I swear fo' God I can't stand that bitch!" I screamed out loud in my car.

I was still sitting in the driveway of my daddy house mad as hell with his stupid ass wife! She had a nerve to come out her mouth reckless at me and put me out of my own daddy's shit? I picked up my phone and tried calling his ass for the fourth time and I still got the voicemail.

"Ugh!" I let out a sigh of frustration as I started my car and drove out of their driveway.

I sent Paul a text message hoping he would make good on his promise and come by and see me later. I was a little low on cash and I needed some money from him, so what better way to get it after I fucked his brains out. I wouldn't have to worry about this shit with my daddy if Fatima would just stay out of my business!

Ever since my mom died when I was young, it has always been my daddy and I. It was safe to say that I was a

43

daddy's girl and loved every minute of it! I got any and everything I wanted from him, and when he was dating women they would try to buy my affection as well. Yea, I took their gifts, but afterwards I would tell my daddy I didn't like them and he would send them on their way.

By the time he introduced me to Fatima, I was well into my teenage years and doing my own thing, so I could care less who he was dating because it kept him out off of my back. She was young and didn't try to smother me like the rest of the women prior to her did. She basically didn't bother me and I was fine with that.

When my dad told me that they were getting married I still didn't care one way or another. By that time I was fucking off the chain and was having fun being able to do what I wanted to do. One night I was at a party and got fucked up off of some weed. I smoked weed before but that shit was totally different from what I was use too! Anyways, the party must have gotten out of control because after I smoked that shit, all I could remember was waking up in a jail cell.

Until this day I don't remember what happened for me to end up there, but lucky for me the cop that apparently arrested me was also member of the church we attended and where my dad was head deacon of and called my father.

Ultimately I got chewed out by my father but the arrest stayed under wraps and never made it to my record because of who my father was. After that incident, I guess he decided to start back paying me some attention instead of Fatima because he became stricter.

I sailed by high school and graduated with the anticipation of getting out of Alexandria and head off to college so I could resume living my life. I went away to Grambling State University in Louisiana and started fucking shit back up again! I was having the time of my life! I was partying my ass off, fucking every fine nigga I came in contact with, drinking, getting high all while still keeping my grades just above average so I didn't have to hear my dad fucking nag.

I majored in business because it was an easy major and I was fucking the dean at that time so I was gonna graduate regardless. But all the fun I had in college, I also had a secret life that no one else knew that I was living. That night at that party back when I was high school changed my life. I ended up graduating college, and it wasn't because I met the requirements either.

The dean wanted to hurry up and get me out off of his campus due to the fact that he was afraid I was gonna expose his ass to his wife. So I graduated, with a proud father and decided instead of staying in Louisiana, I would come back to Ohio. Since I had my degree, my father promised me a lucrative job with his construction company by helping him run it. At first it sounded like a good proposition. Me working alongside my daddy and having guaranteed money, but I found out that was not how things were gonna be.

In reality, I was gonna work for my daddy and not with him. He wanted me start from the bottom and "work my way up" as he put it. He had me on some secretary shit with answering phones, taking messages and signing for some dame packages. Not to mention the pay was starting at $14.00 an hour! Who the fuck could live off that shit?

I know there are people who can live off of less with no choice, but I had a choice and a habit to support. That's right, I said habit. Like I mentioned earlier, that night when I was younger and got fucked up off that weed, I didn't know what the fuck that was. I found out later on that it was laced with heroine.

When I got to Grambling, I was reintroduced to it at a frat party and have been hooked ever since. People thought, including my daddy and his stuck up ass wife that I wanted money to just shop and floss around, but I wanted money to support my habit. I was an addict, but I was a functional one. Don't get it twisted, I love staying laced with the latest and keeping my hair, nails, feet and eyebrows fresh.

Everyone keeps hollering how I need a job and put my fucking degree to use, but why the fuck should I have to work when my daddy was paid and I was fucking the pastor of the biggest church in Ohio! Speaking of Pastors, I noticed that Paul had indeed text me back letting me know that he'll meet me at our spot at 8pm.

Good! Now I can get some dick and some heroine. I'll deal with my daddy and Fatima's ass later!

KARLA

After running into Fatima and her ghetto ass friend, I headed over to Jaspers; which was a boutique we had in Alexandria with the best seamstress this side of the state! It was also where I would have pieces of designer clothes ordered from New York, LA, and Atlanta and have them shipped here to get altered. That's how I stay ahead of these country bitches here.

"So what do you think of this one here?" I asked Marcus as I modeled the dress I just tried on.

"Oh girl, that shit it fierce boo. You wear that inside the church house and you liable to burn that shit down!" Marcus responded being loud and over the top as always.

Marcus was what you would call a queen. Wasn't anything manly about him except the rod between his legs which he tucked so damn good you would swear he already had a coochie; instead of saving up to buy one. "Please, if it hasn't already burned down from Paul trifling ass then I know I'm safe!" I scoffed as I went back into the dressing room to change back into my clothes. While naked, I decided to send Travis a pussy picture just for the hell of it.

"Honey I don't see how you put up with that wolf in sheep clothing!" Marcus said as I was coming back out of the fitting room sitting in the chair waiting on me playing with his freshly manicured nails.

"Don't play coy, you know why I put up with it. Paul is very beneficial, powerful and paid. I stopped caring a long time ago who he was sticking his dick into and started doing me." I replied as I tossed my hair over my shoulders, grabbed my things and headed to the register to have my stuff shipped to my home after the proper alterations were done.

"I know all that sister girl, but it's just too much! I couldn't sit in the front pew every Sunday, smiling and singing praises when I know my husband fucked everyone in the damn congregation" Marcus threw in my face being shady.

I'm really starting to regret telling his ass my damn business because lately it seems like every chance he gets, he's always throwing Paul's indiscretions in my face!

"Well you just let me handle the woman situations and you concentrate on trying to become one" I snorted as I headed out the door to leave with him trailing behind me.

"Excuse me boo! You right though, I'll leave the messiness to you while I concentrate on me and my new boo" Marcus replied as we were walking to my car. I'm so glad he drove his own shit, because he was starting to work my nerves!

"New boo? You haven't told me about any new piece of meat you were seeing. How is he because you know Alexandria ain't that big" I inquired being nosey.

"It sure is, which is why I can't wait to get out of this sardine packed ass town! But anyway, he's nobody you know. He's actually out of town, I met him when I went on one of my excursions to LA six months ago" Marcus said as he licked his tongue out and started winding his hips looking like a damn fool in the parking lot. I couldn't do anything but shake my head at his dramatics.

"LA huh? Hmm, so that means he must be paid?"

"Very!" Marcus grinned.

"Good, then maybe you can put your little coins you were saving for aside and get him to come out the pocket so you can get your kitty cat." I said laughing.

I know I was throwing major shade, but the truth was if anybody else had a come up beside me; I didn't like that shit. I guess you could say I was a jealous bitch.

"Okay, I'm under this shady palm tree thing, but it's

all good. I gotta head out anyway so I'll call you for drinks later on this week" Marcus said as he gave me an air kiss on my left cheek, put his shades on and sashayed to his car.

His ass was portioned perfect with his hips, along with a nice flat stomach and size C cups breast. Marcus had been transitioning to become a woman since the age of 13. He told me the same story you always hear these wanna-be females tell, *I always knew I was a girl trapped in a boy's body* bullshit. Child please I know for a fact that God don't make no mistakes. Yo ass was born a boy with a dick so all that other shit they be saying goes in one ear and out the other.

His momma died when he was three from a drug overdose, and from my understanding his daddy was her pimp and he died in prison from getting stabbed. So he was raised by his grandmother, Mother Earline who has been a long standing member of our church since the beginning of time. She's such a sweet lady and a faithful tithe payer, but I could always tell the disappointment on her face when she sees Marcus in his get up or the mention of his name when folks ask about him.

She always says that she has no heaven or hell to put no one in, and that she loves her grandson unconditionally. But what she wanna say is he needs to sit his sissy ass down somewhere! But back to Marcus, I would be lying if said he wasn't bad because the bitch is bad! Marcus was a natural pretty boy anyway so it wasn't hard for him to be a beautiful woman.

He was red bone complexion, blemish free smooth skin, light hazel eyes, his eye brows and mink lashes stayed on point. He had natural curly texture hair as myself, but he has tamed his hair over the years to a straight texture and keeps it flowing down his back. His bone face structure was so soft and showed no traces of any masculinity and he already had his Adam's apple shaved down so it wouldn't show.

By him taking those estrogen pills faithfully throughout the years, it has really helped him out tremendously. Yea, Marcus was bad and all the women and I'm sure men in Alexandria knew it. When we were out and about, I would catch low key stares from men looking at him. The only thing that was making Marcus transformation fully complete was what was between his legs.

He said that was the final piece for him. I envied Marcus in the background. Not only was he beautiful as ever, but it seemed so simple for him to become whoever he wanted to. Whereas I had to keep up this facade of being the proper first lady with a perfect life and husband. So why am I his friend you're wondering? Well for one, none of these other heffas here in town act like they want to associate with me. They want to be friends with the *First Lady,* not the real me.

I didn't have time to be proper all the time. I cursed, drank and got down when I wasn't in the front row pew. Being with Marcus allowed me to do just that; and also the fact that I can throw my lifestyle and money in his face is a bonus. I pulled out of the parking lot and headed home since Travis hasn't responded to my text message...yet.

PAUL

I couldn't help but laugh at the thought of Travis getting caught up by his wife Fatima. That shit would never happen to me, mainly because Karla knows her place and know who pays those damn credit card bills. But that was the difference between me and Travis, I had my shit in order. I was stopped at the red light when my thoughts started drifting to Fatima.

Ever since Travis introduced her to us at the church, I always wondered what her insides felt like. She was fine as all get out and young! I knew she was new in town at the time because I would have remembered seeing her and I'm pretty sure I would have fucked her, but Travis lucked up and got to her first. If Fatima was that kind of woman, I would still try to bed her ass! But I found out first hand she wasn't. I tried to bait her but she didn't bite.

She loved Travis and from what I know, she knows how he likes to dip in another piece of ass every now and again. I guess she must be getting tired because lately she's been beating women's asses left and right behind him. She was a young sexy ass woman that I wouldn't mind have going crazy over me like that.

Finally the light turned green and I headed home. I didn't know if Karla was there or not and frankly I didn't care. You could say we were living like roommates right now. She stayed on the other side of the house and slept in a separate room from me. I guess you could say we grew apart and only staying married for conveniences. We both know we're not in love with one another anymore, but neither of us has said it out loud. Fifteen minutes later, I punched the code key into my gate and pulled into my circular driveway.

Every time I come home, I'm always reminded how much God has blessed me, or the congregation but they didn't need to know that. I saw that Karla's car was in the driveway as well. I took a deep breath and counted to ten before I got out and made my way inside. Soon as I walked through the door, I found her at the open bar having herself a drink.

"I see you're starting early tonight." I said as I put my keys on the bar and picked up the mail looking through it.

"Hello to you too Paul" Karla mumbled.

Lately it seemed like it pained us to have a decent

conversation with one another.

"Look Karla, what are we doing here?" I finally asked in frustration.

"What are you talking about?"

"I'm talking about this, us" I pointed between the both of us.

"Paul we are fine" she said nonchalantly as she took a sip from her glass.

"No we are not and you know it! We barely say two words to one another when we're in one another's presence, we sleep separately, our sex life is particularly none existence-

"Oh this is about sex?" Karla blurted out cutting me off.

"No it's not just about the sex, but that does play a big part in a marriage Karla. The bible says a wife is supposed to be submissive to her husband; or did you forget that"

"Oh I haven't forgotten it, the problem is my husband has other women being submissive to him already, so what the hell do you need me for?" Karla asked laughing.

"I don't know if it was the liquor talking or not, but you better find some common sense when talking to me" I threatened.

"Oh please, you wanna come in here and try to throw your weight around, asking me why we are the way we are and tell me what the bible says. You know why we're the way we are! You know why I don't have anything to say to you! You know why I sleep on the other side of the house, because you can't keep your dick in your pants! You seem to think I'm that young naïve girl you married back then, but I'm far from that baby!" Karla sneered looking at me with disgust.

I knew she knew what I was doing, but of course I would never openly admit anything.

"So you going off gossip now?" I questioned.

"No, I'm going off facts my dear husband. You think I don't see the stares or whispers from them heffas in the church, or the smell of another woman's cheap ass perfume on you when you walk through this door at night? Or the constant hotel receipts I found when I used to do the laundry. Oh let's not forget the hickey that was on your chest that you swore happened when you were playing golf and the ball *accidently* hit you in the chest! I swear you could come up with stories." Karla laughed again.

"You can say what you want, but we both know that if you would have stayed the wife you were in the beginning then I wouldn't need to have stories to tell you. You see

Karla, no; I don't think you are the same young naïve woman I married. How could you still be her when I groomed you to who you are now? But I see now that you must think you're the shit, but I bet if I snatch those damn credit cards and money access, yo ass will be reminded who you are. So what you need to do is get it together and do what you need to do and get us back on track! Now good night sweet wife." I smiled as I gave her a sloppy kiss on the mouth and walked upstairs.

"You fucking bastard!" I heard Karla yell as glass shattered.

I turned around to see that she had thrown the glass she was drinking from against the wall. I just chuckled as I turned around to head back upstairs. I needed to take a quick shower and make good on my promise to Candice from earlier and tear that pussy up.

TRAVIS

I know Fatima was still pissed at me, because she was giving me the silent treatment at home. This is how it was with us every time she caught me doing my dirt.

"So how was your day baby?" I asked breaking the ice that night at dinner.

It amazes me that even though I constantly messed around, my wife still makes sure she handles her duties.

"Fine" she replied back dryly as she continued to eat her food not showing any interest in me what so ever.

"Look baby, I know you're tired of hearing this, but I'm so sorry" I stated sincerely.

"You are right about two things, yo ass is sorry and I'm tired of hearing it!" Fatima said back to me so calm, yet menacing.

I just stared at her for a while before responding. The look I saw in my wife's eyes showed nothing but hurt and disappointment. I love Fatima, which is why I asked her to be my wife, but I am who I am. No matter how fine and sweet my wife is, how loyal she may remain to me and our marriage, I'm always gone have a supply of pussy on the backburner.

"Fatima it's no need to come out of your mouth so reckless."

"Oh, but it's okay to keep catching my husband with hoes? I swear you are a trip! Travis, I married you with the hope of 'until death do us part', but this shit here is killing me!" Fatima yelled pointing her finger between the both of us. I could see tears threating to fall from her eyes.

"What you mean you can't do this? I hope you're not talking about leaving and divorcing me because that ain't happening." I said to her hoping that she heard me loud and clear.

I vowed that once I married Fatima, that she was going to be my last wife and that I wasn't getting a divorce again; and I meant just that!

"Why, because it'll look bad on the church? How I feel right now, fuck you and that damn church Travis!" she screamed getting up from her seat trying to walk past me. I quickly grabbed her arm tight in passing.

"I told you to watch yo damn mouth, but just like always you so damn hard headed. Now I know I fuck up, but

I also know I take damn good care of you. If you would just concentrate more on us and stop worrying about what the hell I got going on outside of this home, then things would go a lot smoother!"

"Do you hear yourself Travis? I'm not some money hungry chick who married you for your money and stability, I married you because I loved you! I didn't marry you because I see you as a meal ticket Travis. I loved you more than life itself and showed you, but yet that still doesn't seem like enough for you. Six years of the lies, cheating and disrespect. I'm tired of that shit, and I'm tired of you!" Fatima said as she snatched her arm away from me.

"Oh and your rude ass daughter came by here earlier looking for you so you can give her some money I assume. I'm sick of her begging ass too! I swear you both need to be in a damn box together alone." Fatima said as she headed towards the back sliding door leading out to her garden.

That was her own little sanctuary. She had her indoor gazebo and a mini bar set up, surrounded by beautiful roses and flowers that she keeps up. Once she left out the door, I just shook my head and sat back down at the table. Like always, everything Fatima said was true. I know she didn't marry me for my money, hell she had her own when I met her. Working as an ER nurse paid her well, she had her own place, and never asked me for a dime.

But once we said I do, I requested that she quit her job and be a stay at home wife. She also wanted to become a mother since she didn't have any kids of her own, but truthfully I knew that wasn't possible. After Candice's mom died, I didn't want to risk raising another child on my own, so I had a vasectomy. No one knew of this, and I thought about having it reversed once I got with Fatima.

I knew she was a young woman who would want to become a mom one day, but as time went on and I got comfortable, I just put that thought out of my mind. And after about three years of marriage, Fatima just stop mentioning having a child altogether. I reached for my phone in my pocket and pulled it out to call Candice to see what it was that she wanted.

I already knew she wanted money because that's the only time she seems to call me lately. For a long time it was just me and my daughter. Even when I dated from time to time, if she wasn't feeling the woman I was with, then I wasn't either. I surrounded my life around Candice because I knew I was all she had. Then, when I met Fatima, Candice was going into her teenage years and started her rebellious stage.

I really didn't want to deal with her behavior at the

time and just continued to enjoy my relationship with Fatima; with the hopes that Candice would break out of it. That was one of the biggest regrets of my life I have. If I would have grabbed a tighter hold on her then, she wouldn't be like how she is now.

I love my daughter and would give my life for hers, but this is not the way I imagined her to turn out. I paid for a college education and made sure she wanted for nothing and could just focus on her studies. I was the proudest father ever when she walked across that stage to receive her degree in business.

I had hopes of her running my construction company with me in hopes of her taking over one day so I could retire; which is why I wanted her to start from the bottom at my company and work her way up. I wanted her to work hard and not just have it just given to her. But she obviously saw otherwise, because after two months of working there, she quit. After that, she started acting like it was still my responsibility to take care of her.

That's when Fatima finally voiced her opinion and let me know that Candice was a grown woman with a college degree who should be able to support herself, and I couldn't agree with her more on that. So my wallet was tight with Candice, and even though I told her numerous times that it wasn't because of Fatima, she still seems to think that's why I won't give her money like I used to.

The phone rang until her voice mail came on. *Candice, this is your father. Fatima told me you came by earlier so I was calling to check on you on. Call me back when you get this, love you.* Once I hung up the phone, I opened my texts and saw that I had a message from Karla asking me why I haven't responded to her naked pic text from earlier. I erased that message as well. I admit I was still feeling some type of way from things Paul said earlier concerning them two. I got up and headed to the door to see Fatima laid out on her lounge chair in the back. The way she was laid there in the silhouette of the evening sun was a sight to see.

I slowly opened the door and crept out there. As I approached her, I noticed that she had fallen asleep. The dress that she had on slowly crept up her thigh exposing her sexy flesh. My dick instantly started jumping at the sight. I knew around the house Fatima never wore panties, so I got down in front of her and slowly pushed her dress up farther. Once her pussy came into view, I wasted no time diving face first in.

My tongue slid across her click. From the first time I ever tasted Fatima, she always taste like pure strawberries and smelled like clear water down there. I licked my lips and covered her pussy with my wet lips and slithering tongue.

"Hmmm" Fatima stirred in her sleep.

I clamped down on her thighs so she couldn't move, and went to work on eating the fuck out that pussy. Fatima grabbed ahold of the top of my head and she started rotating her hips. That turned me on more as I sucked harder on her pussy. Her juices were trickling down my throat as I swallowing every drop.

As her moans grew louder, I knew she was about to come. Normally I would stop and prepare myself to slide up inside her, but I didn't want to stop the rhythm. Since I know I was in the dog house, I needed to crawl my way out that muthafucka any way I could.

"Oh shit Travis!" Fatima moaned out louder as she grabbed my shoulders.

Seconds later, she released all in my mouth and shaking in the process. Fatima may be younger than me, but since day one I've been putting it down on her ass. I make sure I stamped this pussy whether it's with my dick or tongue. Soon as Fatima stopped shaking, I stood up and wiped my mouth with the back of my hand.

"Get upstairs so I can tear that ass up the right way" I commanded.

Fatima just gave me a look as she stood up herself and headed into the house. I know she was still pissed, but as long as she takes it out on this dick when we get upstairs, we good.

PAUL

"You have heard that it was said, 'Love your neighbor[a] and hate your enemy.' But I tell you, love your enemies and pray for those who persecute you, that you may be children of your Father in heaven. He causes his sun to rise on the evil and the good, and sends rain on the righteous and the unrighteous. If you love those who love you, what reward will you get? Are not even the tax collectors doing that? And if you greet only your own people, what are you doing more than others? Do not even pagans do that? Be perfect, therefore, as your heavenly Father is perfect.

I recited the passage as I was closing out my sermon as I wiped the sweat off my brow. I glanced over at Candice sitting in the third row grinning looking right back at me. I quickly looked away and landed my eyes on Karla, who rolled her eyes at me soon as she saw me. It's crazy of the two different responses I got from my wife and my mistress.

"Now I want you all to bow your heads as Deacon

Whitehead closes us out" I announced as I took my seat back in the pulpit as Travis came up to the altar.

As everyone's head was bowed and eyes closed in prayer, I looked up to notice Karla's eyes wide open grinning in the direction of Travis. *What the hell* I thought to myself. I was by far a dumb man, and the look I saw in Karla's eyes was nothing but lust. I sat there and watched her as she watched him without noticing me. I started getting hot under my robe. I pulled at my collar to loosen up some.

Until now, I never noticed anything with Karla and another person, let alone Travis. Soon as Travis was done with the closing prayer, I dismissed the congregation. As usual, Karla and I took our place next to the exit and shook hands with those leaving.

"That was a very nice sermon Pastor" Candice said as I shook her hand.

The way she was smiling in my face and not acknowledging Karla was very noticeable.

"Thank you dear, but you have to keep moving because we have others that need to get by" Karla interrupted.

Candice just looked at her and rolled her eyes as she released my hand and left out the door. I cut my eye over at Karla and saw that she was beyond pissed. I continued to see the rest of the parishioner's out ignoring the nasty looks she kept giving me. Soon as I saw Travis and Fatima come into view, my hands began to get sweaty.

Fatima looked so sexy in her navy blue skirt suit that hugged all her curves. Her hair flowed down her back with a part down the middle, and she had traces of very little make up on her face. But I do admit, that red lipstick she was wearing on her plum lips made my dick pulsate in my pants. *Lord please forgive me for these thoughts I'm having.* I silently prayed to myself.

"Great sermon Pastor" Fatima acknowledged as she hugged me.

Her smell was so intoxicating and as her cheek brushed up against mines, I could feel how soft her skin was. I cut my eye over at Karla and Travis' interaction and the way Karla was now smiling in his face only made me suspicious even more.

"Thank you Sister Whitehead. How is everything with you, I haven't seen you already at bible study lately" I inquired.

Normally, I move folks along so I could hurry up and greet the next person, but for some reason I wanted to stand there and talk to Fatima a little linger.

"Oh I'm sorry. I've just been a little busy at home,

but I promise I'll make time for future bible studies" Fatima assured me flashing that beautiful smile of hers.

"Well I'm going to hold you to that. I won't hold you two up, so have a nice evening guys" I said quickly as I grabbed Travis' hand and shook it.

After we finished seeing everyone off and the money was counted for today, Karla and I headed home. On the drive home, we were both quiet, and normally I would welcome this silence but not today.

"So you ready to tell me what the hell is going on with you and Travis?" I blurted out.

"What!" Karla asked surprised as she snapped her head in my direction.

I continued to look straight ahead as I was driving, but I could see her stare from out of the corner of my eye.

"You heard what I said" I replied.

"Look, just because you have that bitch Candice drooling all over your ass, don't try and throw accusations my way" Karla shot back at me obviously trying to switch this around on me.

"Whatever Candice do ain't got shit to do with me, now I'm going to ask you again, what the fuck is going on with you and Travis?"

Karla chuckled before answering me. "You are a trip

Paul, but to answer your question, not a damn thing."

"You must take me for some fool. I noticed today how every time you looked his way you were blushing like a damn school girl; and we both know you are far from that" I insulted.

I know I did my dirt on my wife, but the thought of her being with another man had me pissed.

"Like I said, nothing is going on" was all Karla said as she looked out the passenger window.

The rest of the ride home was quiet with both of us deep in our thoughts. Once we pulled up in the driveway, Karla immediately jumped out and slammed the door as she stormed inside the house. I cut the car off and went inside greeted with the smell of our Sunday dinner prepared by our chef.

My stomach started growling as I headed upstairs to change out of my clothes so I could eat. Soon as I got into our bedroom, I heard the shower running. I opened the door to see Karla letting the water beat down on her body. For her to be over the age of forty, her body was still tight and intact. Although I was still mad about earlier, I wasn't about to turn away from getting some pussy.

I quickly stripped out of my clothes and slid the shower door open.

"What are you doing in here?" Karla asked startled.

I didn't say anything as I took her loofa from her, turned her around and started slowly washing her back. I washed slowly in a circular motion all around her back. I then traveled down to the top of her ass crack. I dropped the loofa and got down on my knees and replaced it with my tongue.

I started sucking on her ass cheeks as I was tightly gripping them. I stood up and turned Karla around so that her back was against the shower wall and got back down on my knees in front of her. With her right leg hiked up over my shoulder and the water beating down on my back, I started sucking on her pussy lips. Karla had one hand pressed against the wall as the other was gripping the top of my head.

I fucked her with my tongue as I stuck it in and out of her pussy. I then stood up and turned her around to face the wall and plunged my dick inside her opening.

"Ahh" Karla moaned out. Although it's been a while since we had sex, her pussy still fit like a glove around my dick.

I grabbed ahold of her hair from the back as I started fucking the shit out of her. I had my eyes closed, and pictured that it was Fatima I was inside instead of my wife. Karla started throwing it back and talking shit, but I tuned her out as I was still imaging that it was Fatima I was fucking.

Karla started trembling which let me know that she was cumming. I sped up my rhythm and within minutes I released all my seeds inside of her. Karla pushed me out of her and made her way in front of me so she could wash off. I leaned up against the wall trying to catch my breath as I watched her wash herself off. Seconds later she got out the shower without saying a word to me.

Selfish ass bitch, didn't even have the courtesy to wash my dick off. I thought to myself as I grabbed my cloth and took a quick shower. Once I was done showering, I dried off and went into our bedroom to see that Karla wasn't there. I put on some sweats and a t shirt and headed downstairs to eat.

CANDICE

Paul was looking so sexy standing in the pulpit earlier. I kept looking at his ass biting on my bottom lip reminiscing on what he did to me the night before. Paul and I met up and fucked until the wee hours of the morning! I was high also, so that made the sex even better. But before last night Paul had no idea I got high.

Paul sent me a message earlier telling me to meet me at our spot so he could made good on his promise. Soon as I saw his message, I got a tingle between my thighs. I quickly jumped in my car and headed out. I had to make a quick stop real quick to get my *candy.* Once I copped, I made my way to the hotel and went to take a quick shower before Paul got there.

Soon as I was done showering, I wrapped myself up in a towel on sat down on the toilet. I grabbed my spoon, lighter, syringe and my foil of dope. I opened it up and poured it into my spoon, and then set fire under it. Looking at the heroine fizzle on the spoon made my mouth water.

Once it was finished, I hit the center of my right arm to locate a vain. Once it appeared, I filled the needle with the content and injected it into my veins. As I felt it flow thru my veins, I leaned back against the toilet with my eyes closed as I prepared to float. I was so out of it that I didn't even hear Paul burst into the door.

"What the fuck is this!" Paul yelled standing in the bathroom doorway causing me to open my eyes.

I tried to sit up, but my body felt so heavy.

"Hey baby, I didn't hear you when you came in" I said smiling and talking low.

"Candice what the hell are you doing with a fucking needle sticking out of your damn arm? Are you getting high?" Paul yelled as he walked inside the bathroom and snatched the needle out of my arm.

"Ouch!" I yelled in pain as blood started to trail down my arm.

I grabbed the towel that was wrapped around me and cleaned the blood off of my arm.

"I can't believe this shit! I can't be fucking with no damn junkie Candice!" Paul said as he grabbed me by my shoulders and stood me up.

"I'm not a damn junky Paul, calm down. I just like to

get a little high from time to time so it's no big deal" I proclaimed as I snatched away from him.

"I can't tell, look at this shit! Paul yelled pointing at my things on the sink.

He was starting to blow my high and I couldn't have that, so I reached down and unbuckled his pants and roughly pulled them down with his briefs at the same time. I slowly dropped to my knees and took his chocolate stick all the way inside my mouth. I knew good head would shut his ass up.

I started licking and slurping up and down his dick as I spit on it from time to time only to lick it back off. I was my horniest when I was high and Paul wasn't about to ruin that. I started jerking his dick as I continued to suck it with both hands. Paul had to grip the edge of the sink to hold his composure. I was sucking his dick like I had an automatic suction in my damn mouth.

When I felt Paul thrusting his hips faster, I knew he was about to cum. I grabbed the tip of his dick with my lips and continued to suck harder as he released in my mouth. I made sure not to waste a drop.

I stood up as Paul was still trying to catch his breath, and turned around as I hiked my leg on the edge of the sink and tooted my ass in the air waiting for him to slide in me. I felt Paul jam himself hard inside of me.

"Fuck!" I yelled out in pure pleasure as I leaned my head back.

Paul gripped both of my shoulders from behind and started drilling my pussy. Between this hard core fucking and the dope, I was on a cloud of its own!

"Fuck this, get yo ass in the bed." Paul ordered as he pulled his dick out of me and slapped me on my ass.

I hurried inside the room and laid on the bed spread eagle, waiting for him to dive in. Paul came right behind me, now fully naked and climbed on top of me. Normally I would expect some passionate foreplay from him, but he just rammed his dick straight inside me; straight fucking.

"Damn baby slow down" I moaned as I tried to keep up with his pace.

"Shut up and take this dick!" Paul grunted as he thrust harder.

His cockiness turned me on even more. My pussy started flooding with my juices as I matched his rhythm with throwing it back just as hard. Paul always had some good dick; that was never the problem. The problem was he just had to give this good muthafucka to every bitch that wanted it other than his wife!

"Turn that ass over and let me fuck you in it" Paul asked as he slid back out of me and positioned himself on his knees in the bed.

I was hesitant at first because I hated this shit. For about a year now, Paul had this fetish of fucking me in the ass. I mean we have done some freaky shit, but this one was my least favorite. But I couldn't deny him his pleasures with me. I got up and got on my knees on the bed as well with my ass up in the air.

I arched my back as I felt Paul tongue sliding across my asshole as lubricant. Seconds later I felt the stinging sensation as he entered my hole.

"Ouch." I yelled out as I tried to move forward.

"Uh huh, don't move" Paul said as he gripped tighter onto my hips and pushed himself farther inside.

It felt like my insides were being ripped apart! Although I could never get use to this pain, it seemed worse since we haven't done it in a while. I put my face down in the pillow to stifle out my cries, that way he wouldn't go harder.

"Yeah, that right take this shit! You like this dick don't you?" Paul clenched out loud as he kept drilling in my ass.

The pain was starting to really become unbearable and I just wanted it over with, so I said what he wanted to hear in order for that to happen.

"Yes baby, this dick is so damn good! Cum for me

daddy!" I commanded as I lifted my head up from the pillow and started moaning loud.

Just as I predicted, minutes later Paul grunted loudly as he released his loads in me. I was so glad this shit was over with, but I knew I would be feeling this pain for a while after this. Finally, Paul pulled out of me and got up and went into the bathroom. I heard the shower running again which lets me know he was taking a shower.

I slowly got up out of the bed and dragged myself to one of our guest bathroom across the way, naked and all. I didn't want to risk taking a shower with Paul again because I knew it would lead to round two, and I couldn't take that right now.

FATIMA

Travis thought that just because I let him taste me the other day, that things between us were back good; but that was far from the case. I meant what I said by being tired of his shit. I was finally at a point where I felt like I gave my marriage 100% only to keep getting the same results from him in return.

I didn't know coming to a small town would cause me bigger grief than before. I knew I needed a plan to get away from here, Travis and that damn church! Speaking of church, I swear Pastor Paul was a fucking nasty bastard! It's no secret of his numerous affairs and infidelities he has around town and within the church. I'm no fool, the way he looks at me, constantly giving me compliments and finding any excuse to touch me are beginning to be too much!

At first I would brush it off, but as time grew it just kept being constant. I knew given the chance he would try to fuck me, and even though my husband is a bona-fide hoe, I still refused to cheat on my marriage. I strongly believe that at all costs, that a woman must remain just that, a woman. I decided to call Tonya to see what she was up to.

"What's up chick?" she greeted me as she answered the phone on the second ring.

"Nothing much. Just not too long ago got in from church and I'm more stressed than I was before going there this morning!" I admitted.

"Girl I told you that ain't no damn church, that's a damn cult with a horny ass preacher!" Tonya laughed into the phone.

I joined her laughing because that shit was funny.

"Speaking of which, he called himself trying to low-key make a pass at me again. Only this time Travis and Karla was standing there!!"

"I swear his ass has no shame, and his dumb ass wife is just as clueless" Tonya responded.

"She may not be as clueless as people think, I mean it's not like the shit he does is a secret, hell none of them are." I sighed thinking about my own fucked up situation.

"Whether she knows it or not, there is nothing worse than a woman knowingly being a fool for a man. I don't give a damn how much money he has!" Tonya said with a yawn.

"Somebody must have been out late" I chuckled.

"Yea, working. One of the other nurses quit so I have to cover her shift until we find somebody else and this night shift is kicking my ass" she explained. "I really wish you would come back to work, it'll be just like old times with us and it'll keep your mind occupied for a while."

I was thinking long and hard about what she was saying. Truth was, I really missed working and I knew that would occupy my time until I could figure out what it was I was going to do. I knew Travis would probably still object to me working, but that was just a conversation we were just gonna have.

"I think you're right." I finally answered.

"For real?" Tonya asked excited into the phone.

"Yeah."

"Oh shit, my girl back!" Tonya sang into the phone.

I couldn't do anything but shake my head and laugh at her crazy self.

"Listen, I'm going to call Evelyn right now and let her know that you want to come to work. I'll text you back with what she says, and don't be bullshitting!" Tonya warned.

Evelyn was our Supervisor and the head Nurse and had a fit when I resigned from there.

"I'm serious this time Tonya" I reassured her.

"What about Travis, you know he's gonna trip" She reminded me.

"I'll handle him, besides it's not up to him anymore. This is my life and I'm taking it back."

"That's what I'm talking about! Okay, I'll call Evelyn and hit you back."

"Okay you do that" I said as I hung up the phone.

I got up from the couch and went into the kitchen to check on my Sunday dinner and pour me a drink to calm my nerves. I heard Travis' footsteps coming down the stairs and into the kitchen.

"Dinner will be ready in a minute" I informed him soon as he came into the kitchen.

"It smells good in here baby, I can't wait to eat." Travis said as he tapped me lightly on my butt.

"Go ahead and set the table for us" I asked him as I cut the stove off and took the roast out of the oven.

Once Travis set the table, I filled our plates of roast, macaroni and cheese, pigeon peas and rice, sweet corn, and strawberry cheesecake muffins. I poured us my home maid sweet lemonade and we took our seats. Soon as Travis blessed the food we dug in.

"Church was good today" Travis spoke breaking the silence.

"Yeah" Was all I said.

"What's wrong with you?" Travis questioned staring at me.

I decided that now was the time to bring up me going back to work.

"Travis, I've been thinking long and hard and I decided that I want to go back to work at the hospital" I said looking at him in his face so I could see his reaction.

Travis just sat there chewing on his food and looking back at me before speaking.

"I thought we already had this discussion and it was decided that I wanted my wife to stay at home" Travis spoke as he wiped his mouth with his napkin.

"No actually *we* didn't discuss anything. It was a demand you made in the beginning of our marriage and I went with it. But enough time has passed and things have obviously changed and I'm ready to go back to work" I replied standing my ground.

"What has changed Fatima?" he questioned as if he really didn't have a damn clue.

"Us Travis" I answered him back rolling my eyes.

This was a conversation I definitely didn't feel like having, it was like a damn boomerang when it came to this; but the truth was the truth. We both just continued to sit there and eat in silence. The tension was so thick that you could slice it with a knife. Suddenly I heard Travis clear his throat.

"You know what baby, you're right. It wasn't a discussion between the both of us. I made that decision for you and you obliged. I shouldn't have taken that from you because I know how much you love nursing, so if you want to go back to work I don't mind" Travis said sincerely.

I had to look around the room to see if I was being punked! This was not the reaction I was expecting from him. I was prepared to go to war about this and let his ass have it, but I just got thrown a loop!

"Wow, I appreciate that" was all I could muster up.

"You deserve whatever it is you want. The things I have been putting you through make you worthy of anything, and I know you're tired of hearing this but I am deeply sorry Fatima" Travis said as he reached over and grabbed my hand looking me in my eyes.

If he would have said this to me a couple of years back, I would be putty in his hands. But I grew to know better. The only surprising thing is him agreeing for me to go back to work.

"So you must be bored with your latest bitch" I blurted out.

"What?" Travis coughed as he was drinking from his

glass.

"You heard me. Come on Travis, every time you get caught with your dick in another bitch you always try to stay in my good graces afterward. Then once you feel like things are back to normal with us you go back to being the whore you are" I snickered as I took a sip of my own drink.

"I suggest you watch your mouth on the Lord's Day Fatima."

"Oh so you want me to wait until tomorrow to tell you the truth? Fine I can wait."

"No, what I want is for you to let the past go so we can move on! I know I messed up-

"No you keep messing up!" I interrupted him.

Suddenly his phone went off indicating he had a message. He didn't respond back to me, but immediately tended to his phone. This nigga had a nerve to have a smirk on his face when he was reading whatever it was in his phone. I was tempted to snatch that shit and throw it upside his head!

"I'm not about to have this conversation again Fatima. I thought we moved on from this but obviously you still want to be on it. I'm about to head over to the site real quick and sign some paperwork for some deliveries we have coming in and get a head start on payroll. I'll see you later tonight." With that said, Travis got up and kissed me on the forehead and headed out to leave.

Moments later I heard the front door close. *What the fuck just happened here!* I said out loud as I still continued to sit there. Now the old me would have protested him leaving and then follow his ass, but I was tired. Mentally and physically. I reached for my own phone and text Tonya letting her know that it was official.

She replied back with the dancing emoji and suggested that we go out for drinks tonight to celebrate. At first I was hesitant, but thought what the hell. Shit it was obvious that Travis' ass was gone to get his next piece of ass so I might as well go out and enjoy myself. I might even find me a lil piece of action myself! Yeah right, who am I kidding, that's not even how I roll.

I text her back letting her know that I was game. She wanted to go to this jazz lounge called Euphony that was located about forty-five minutes outside of town. I was down for that because I didn't want to see these folks around here anyway. We agreed that she would pick me up around 8pm and I would ride with her.

I looked at the clock and saw that I had about three hours to waste before she got here, so I put the rest up the food up; washed up the dishes and headed upstairs to soak in a nice hot bath before I got my drink on.

TRAVIS

I was happy as hell when I got the text from Sabrina telling me that she had just got into town and wanted to taste me. My dick instantly jumped at the thought of her mouth wrapped around the head of my dick. Sabrina was a woman that I met about two months ago when she came over to my office to drop off the invoices from this new supply company I was using. She was the owner's niece and working as his secretary for the summer.

The moment I saw Sabrina walk through my door with that round juicy ass, her breasts sitting upright and in sight, and juicy lips; I knew I had to have her. She was also younger than me, by about ten years. I may have been an older dude, but the way I was built and my swag would give any young dude a run for their money! How do you think I snatched up Fatima like I did? Shit I stay in the gym and eating right with the occasional soul food Sunday dinner.

Sabrina wasn't from here, she was from Atlanta and

was here visiting her folks for the summer. She was built like a damn stallion and it showed when we fucked too! She flirted heavy with me the first time we met and I knew right then and there I could get her; which I did. That day when she dropped off the invoices, we exchanged numbers and met up that exact same night where I we fucked until my dick was raw!

Afterwards, we would occasionally hook up while she was here until she left to go back home with the promise of coming back soon. I had no problem with that because her not being here full-time made it easier for me to deal with my wife, Karla, and whoever else I felt like it. Speaking of Karla, she had been blowing up mu phone like crazy. The only time I spoke to her was when we were leaving church and we greeted them on the way out. Shit, I was wondering what she wanted so badly with me when her husband made it clear that he was still fucking her every which way.

I mean don't get me wrong, I know Paul is her husband and entitled to tear it up whenever he gets ready too, I just don't appreciate her lying to me telling me that they sleep separately and haven't had sex in the last five months. Shit, no need to lie to try to make me feel better because it's not like I tell her ass I ain't fucking Fatima. Matter of fact I don't even mention my wife to her or any other woman I deal with. Fatima is off limits and I make that clear up front with them so there won't be any misunderstandings.

I still haven't been responding to her messages or calls, I decided to deal with her later. Right now I needed to make peace at home, which is why I agreed to Fatima finally going back to work. I figured that'll keep her off my back and I could continue doing me. I knew after a while though, Karla would start acting jealous and shit if I kept ignoring her, but she'll be alright.

Thirty minutes later I pulled into the Radisson parking lot and text her letting her know that I was there. She replied with the room number and I headed that way. Once I got on the floor and knocked on the door, Sabrina answered it naked with a glass of champagne in her hand.

"Hey daddy, I missed you" She greeted me as she pulled me into the room and slid her tongue in my mouth.

She tasted like sweet strawberries.

"Hmm I missed you too baby, Damn!" I said as I bit her bottom lip and slapped her naked ass.

Why don't you get out of those clothes and come soak in the tub with me. I already have it waiting for us and you can start there by showing me how much you miss me" she said seductively as she started unbuckling my pants.

Sabrina may have been young, but she was trained!

She was a stripper back in Atlanta before deciding to want better of her life, so she's been around the block before. She never asked me was I married even though I always wore my band faithfully, she never nagged me, and always waited until I contacted her first before we talked; with the exception of now letting me know that she was here.

We had fun with no questions asked or no promises made and that's the way I liked it. Soon as I was fully undressed, I followed Sabrina into the bathroom where a big round Jacuzzi tub was full of water and bubbles with candles lit around it.

"I see somebody was waiting on Daddy" I said as I slid into the hot water and held my hand out for her to get in.

"I told you I missed you baby, what have you been up to?" Sabrina questioned as she sat between my legs and grabbed the loofa.

"The usual, working and church" I responded as I took the loofa out of her hand and started washing her back with it.

"I still can't believe you're a deacon" Sabrina laughed.

"Why not?"

"Well first off, you don't look like one. The deacons I grew up seeing were old and looked like they already had one foot in the grave. And second you just don't act like it" she explained.

"How do deacons act?" I questioned as I started rubbing her breast in a circular motion as she laid back against my chest.

"Definitely not like this" she said as she turned around and positioned herself on top of me in a squat position on top of me.

I lifted her up lightly as I grabbed ahold of my dick so she could slid down on it which is exactly what she did.

"Shit" I whispered out loud as I felt the mixture of her tight pussy and the warm water.

I started biting on her nipples and she bounced up and down on my dick. Between the sounds of the water splashing and moans, we were making fucking music. This was the first time I didn't use a condom with Sabrina or any other woman I fucked outside of my wife with the exception of Karla because her ass had a hysterectomy and I didn't have to worry about having any mishaps with her. Although I had a vasectomy, there were still diseases out here and I definitely couldn't deal with that!

I knew I was fucking up by not using protection with Sabrina, but this pussy was too good to climb out off! We fucked for about twenty minutes in the tub, with her coming back to back. She finally stood up and let the water out of the tub and cut the shower on so we could rinse off.

Once we were done, we took the action into the room where I threw her on the bed and proceeded to finish what I started in the tub. I grabbed both of her legs and pinned them behind her head and up against the headboard and started pounding the hell out of her pussy! Again, I didn't have protection on, but at this point I just didn't give a damn.

"That's right baby, get this shit!" Sabrina yelled out as she tried to thrust her hips to match my rhythm.

She was making her pussy walls grip my dick and that alone was making me about to cum. I wanted to pull out of her but somehow Sabrina freed her legs from my grip and had them wrapped tightly around my hips. *Fuck it!* I thought to myself as I sped up the pace and finally came.

Suddenly I felt a real wet substance, I pulled out of her to see what looked like sperm dripping from the head of my dick. I don't know if it was Sabrina's juices or what, but I started to panic badly!

MARCUS

It's funny how Karla's stick figure ass thinks she's so much better than me. I peeped game a long time ago with her ass! The only reason I put up with her is to make sure I have tabs on the bitch like I'm supposed too! That's right, I'm not really that bitch's friend or *personal shopper* as she has these country ass folks thinking.

Matter of fact, I'm fucking her man! You heard me right, I'm fucking Reverend Paul Stanley and enjoying every bit of it! I know folks think I'm messy for doing this, but so what! I hate bitches who always think their shit don't stink and look their noses down on other people; and that's exactly how Karla's ass is!

Anyways, Paul and I hooked up a couple of months back when he went to North Carolina for a conference and I was there visiting this other trade that I hook up with from time to time. Unless I told you, you couldn't tell that I was really a man.

I was flawless honey from my head down to my size seven feet! Growing up as a little boy in this country ass town, I was always called a pretty boy, faggot and sissy. I never played with the boys or got dirty. I knew I was different when I always wanted to do the exact same things the girls wanted to do. Hell I would cry when I wasn't invited to their sleepovers! I didn't care that it was for girls only, shit I considered myself one of the girls.

My momma was always hoeing around and got into drugs, and I'm not sure about my daddy so my grandma raised me. Even though I knew she didn't approve of my lifestyle, she has always been here for me and loved me unconditionally. So as I got older, I knew that if I wanted to become the woman I was meant to be, that I needed to leave Alexandria and broaden my horizons.

Soon as I graduated high school, I left the next day with the graduation money my grandma gave me, and the money I had saved up from working and hauled ass. I always wanted to go to LA so I went there. I had no idea what I was going to do there and knew no one. I had a total of $3,700 to my name. I got a lil efficiency I rented from this old couple that was located in back of their house. Next, I ended up getting a job as a bar tender in a strip club called Clermont Lounge where I met folks and learned all the tricks of the trade.

I was still newly transitioning then to become a woman, so people still knew I was a man. But I was a pretty man with light complexion, natural curly hair, hazel eyes and slim build. I was taking the hormone pills but I felt they were moving too slow. But never the less, I was accepted for who I was. The shit I was going through wasn't uncommon there anyway.

As time grew, everyone that came into the club knew who Marcus was. Some of the baddest strippers in the club took me under their wing and that's when I started blossoming into the bad bitch of a woman I am. I was still bartending where I was making good ass money, but my side hustle is what put me over the top. I started meeting dudes who were fascinated by my looks and wanted to fuck me. So I let them know that they had to pay in order to play with me.

Within six months of being in LA, I had moved into a two bedroom condo and pushing a brand new Infinity truck. You would be shocked at how many athletes, husbands, lawyers, doctors, that I had filling up my pockets and sucking my dick in the process. By then I had my titties and ass done to the perfect proportion. I also had my Adams apple shaved down so it wouldn't be noticeable. I made sure I worked out religiously to keep my stomach and abs intact also.

I made sure my hair stayed laid with my routine sew in of Malaysian; and I faithfully stayed getting my manicure, pedicure and eyebrows threaded every two weeks. I had transformed into a woman that real women wanted to be like. The only thing that really confirmed that I was a man was what was swinging between my legs. Getting my dick snipped was gonna be the last thing I did to be complete, but it seemed like the men I was with loved the fact that I had it and paid more, so I just put that on the back burner.

While I was doing my thing in LA, I made sure to send money back home to my grandma. She took care of me without one complaint and I was gonna make sure that she wanted for nothing. She would always say how she wanted me to come home to visit, but I would always come up with an excuse as to why I couldn't.

Truth was, Alexandria was suffocating and I didn't want to go back there no time soon. The only reason I'm back here now is because my grandma was diagnosed with breast cancer and I'm here to take care of her.

Back to the Pastor. I was in North Carolina meeting up with a dude I had dealt with from time to time. He was a judge that liked to get freaky as hell and have his ass licked. He flew me out there for a weekend fuck fest between us. The hotel we were scheduled to stay in just happened to be holding the conference that Paul was attending.

I guess the good judge didn't know that when he booked it, because once my plane landed I got the text saying he couldn't risk being seen and that I could stay there for the weekend since the room was already paid for. He also said he would try to come over late night for my little goodies and still pay me like he promised.

Initially I was pissed that I had come all this way for nothing, but when I saw that he made good on his word and deposit $5,800 into my bank account, I was satisfied. I decided to head over to the hotel and just chill for the weekend since I was already here.

Imagine my surprise when I bumped into Paul getting off the elevator heading to my room. Of course he didn't recognize me, but I knew exactly who he was. He was fine as ever and made my dick jump when I saw him. Paul being the hoe that he was known to be, flirted with me and asked for my number so we could catch up later.

I laughed as I stood there listening to him trying to run game on me, not knowing I already knew what time it was with him. We exchanged numbers, and that night when I was settled in Paul sent me a text asking if he can come by my room for a drink. Drink my ass, but I told him he could. Soon as he came to my room, he tried to play coy and ask me a bunch of questions as if he was trying to get to know me.

"What is it that you want from me Paul, you want to fuck; because if you do I have no problem with that" I blurted out to him not beating around the bush.

"Well you waste no time in knowing what you want do you?" he laughed nervously.

"Time is something I hate to waste besides money" I said shrugging my shoulders as I got up and went to get me a bottle of Patron from the mini bar.

"I agree with that" Paul said as he came up from behind me and wrapped his arms around my waist.

His touch felt so good and secure. I turned around to face him where I was greeted with his tongue going down my throat. Now, normally I wouldn't kiss men I was fucking with in the mouth. It seemed too personal and I was only dealing with them for business purposes only. But it was something about Paul. I think the fact he was a Pastor in my home town had an effect in that. We stood there and kissed passionately for about a few good minutes before I pulled away.

"Paul there is something I need to let you know" I said moving back from him so we could have some distance between us.

"What you married, because if you are I don't care

about that" he responded panting.

"No, that would be you" I said pointing to his ring. "As you already know, I'm not the one to sugarcoat shit or beat around the bush. What you see with me is what you get, and if you don't want it, trust me there's plenty of niggas who do."

"I'm not understanding." Paul shook his head in confusion.

I slowly walked back towards him and grabbed his right hand. I then put it on my breast and started slowly sliding down over my stomach until I reached my thighs. I stopped for a moment and then proceeded until I reached my middle. I positioned myself so that my dick could unravel and moved his hand there.

Soon as Paul felt it his eyes got big from my surprise, but ironically he didn't remove his hand. We both just stood there in silence trying to figure out what the next move would be. Paul suddenly grabbed me towards him and started kissing me again. That right there was confirmation that he was down for the cause with me.

He fucked me so good that day and has been ever since. I later revealed to him that I knew who he was and who my grandmother was, but he still didn't care. Long as I kept what was between us hush, he was cool with that. I went back to LA and continued on with my business until I had to come back here.

That Sunday when I attended church with my Grandma, the stares and whispers from folks didn't mean shit to me. Matter of fact, I found it hilarious. But the look on Paul's face when he saw me was a sight to see! He looked like he saw a ghost when service was over and we greeted him and his funky ass wife as we were leaving. Later on that night, I got a text asking me to meet up with him at a hotel on the outskirts.

When I got there, he started drilling me with questions as to why I was here and what were my intentions. I had to put him in his place real quick and let his ass know that I was here for my grandma and not his ass. Soon as he was convinced, we picked up where we left off and continued to fuck around. So like I said earlier, Karla has no idea that I'll always have one up on here and that her man likes my dick better than her coochie.

I was on my way to meet with Paul at our spot now for a little afternoon rendezvous. When I pulled up, I saw his car already there letting me know he was waiting for me inside. I knocked lightly on the door and waited for him to answer.

"About time you got here" he said as he snatched the

door open and ushered me in while looking to see if anyone saw me.

I swear his ass can be so damn dramatic at times. From the pulpit to this shit.

"Whatever, I had to make sure my granny was straight before I left. Anyways I hope you have something to drink because I forgot to stop on the way over there" I said as I made my way over to the bed and took my shoes off to get comfortable.

"I don't have anything to drink, but I think I have something better." He exclaimed grinning as he made his way over to the bed and stood over me.

I look to see that he had a small bag with some powder in it. I was far from dumb so I already knew what it was, the question since when did his ass get down like this?

"What the hell is that?" I asked trying to get clarification on what it was.

"This right here is that smack that's gonna have me fucking the dog shit out yo ass!" he answered licking his lips.

"Heroine? Since when did you start using that shit?"

"I don't, I just use it for special occasions like now" he said as he started sucking on my neck while rubbing on my dick.

I dibbled and dabbled with some coke and weed from

time to time in LA, but never heroine. Paul stood up and went over to the desk table and pulled out the rest of his contents. I sat there on the bed and watched him as he poured the heroine onto the spoon and lit it. He then pulled out his needle and syringe and went to work with shooting up. For someone who doesn't do this, he damn sure knew exactly what it was he was doing.

I sat there stunned as I watched Paul get high. Soon as he was done, he walked back over to me. He grabbed my arms and led me to stand up. He then pulled the skirt that I was wear down and a reached to pull my dick from being tucked. He started jacking me slowly and he licked up and down my caramel stick. I leaned my head back and exhaled in pleasure and I felt the warmth of his mouth.

I may have transformed into a woman, but my dick still reacted to touch. He got down on his knees and went to work on my dick. I grabbed ahold of the back of his head and started fucking his mouth.

"That's right, swallow my shit" I commanded.

Paul opened his mouth wider deep throating me whole. I never had a man suck my dick off the way Paul was at this moment, I guess his little pick me up brings the freak out of him more.

KARLA

It's been a while since Paul and I fucked, and I admit the shit was good! But that still doesn't change things between us and the fact that Travis got his ass beat in the dick department. Speaking of Travis, he has been acting real funny with me lately since the last time we hooked up. I text and call him but he never responds, and when I saw him at church I didn't know that I was making it that obvious that I was happy to see him for Paul to notice.

This was the first time that he ever acknowledged or acted jealous about my interaction with another man, and I admit I kind of liked it. Little does he know though, it goes deeper than that with me and Travis. If I had it my way he would be my husband instead of Paul. Maybe Paul was trying to keep the peace at home with Fatima, which is why he's acting distance right now. It wouldn't be the first time he would have done this, so I would sit back and wait for him to come back to this good-good right here.

I had a meeting tonight with the Women of Empowerment at the church and really didn't feel like going. It was a group designed by me when I first became the first lady to help empower women. We started out having weekly meetings and coming up with ideas and fundraisers so that we can indulge in activities amongst us.

There were a lot of young ladies that joined the group and became very helpful and insightful. Since I started everything, it was natural that I was president. The group had been going strong up until two years ago when I found out Paul was fucking one of the young girls in the group. It seemed like everyone else knew but me and feeling like a fool was an understatement! I was in the bathroom one day at the church after we had just wrapped up a meeting. It was around Christmas time and we had finalized our plans for our annual toy drive.

So I'm the bathroom, in the stall handling my business when I hear someone come in.

"Oh my God Tish, what are you going to do?" I heard someone say.

"I have no idea, but I don't want to make Paul upset" I heard the other voice say.

My ears instantly started burning at the mention of the names and the recognition of the voice. I remained on the toilet quiet and struggled to peak through the little slit from my stall to see if I could see anyone. Sure enough it was the two young ladies from my group Tish and her side kick Moni. They both were high school seniors and hot in the ass!

Both of their parents thought that it would be a good idea to have them join the group for some guidance. I continued to sit there and eaves drop on their conversation. Never did I think they were talking about my Paul, I mean these are children for God's sake!

"Listen, the Pastor has more than enough money to handle this. Besides, him getting mad should be the least of your problems" I heard Moni say.

Right then and there I saw red as I got my confirmation that they were talking about my husband! I quickly stood up and wiped myself and I pulled down my dress, and burst out of the stale. The girls both looked shocked and knew they had been busted.

"I need to talk to Tish alone for a minute Moni" I said to Moni as I stared at Tish.

Moni looked hesitant for a minute while looking back and forth between Tish and me, and finally left out the bathroom. Once Moni left out, Tish just stood there like the little girl she was with her head held down in shame.

"So If I heard correct, you were talking about my

husband. What is it that he would mad about Tish?" I questioned as I stood there with my arms folded across my chest waiting for an answer.

Immediately tears started falling down her face. "I'm so sorry First Lady, I really am" she started sobbing.

She placed her hands over her stomach and started crying some more. I stood there in a trance as I already knew what was going on. My husband was fucking this child who had become pregnant by him. She didn't even have to say it anything, her actions spoke it to me.

"You might as well wipe those damn tears because you damn sure wasn't crying when you were fucking my husband!" I seethed through my teeth.

She shot her head up and looked at me in astonishment like she couldn't believe what I had just said. Here I was the First Lady, her mentor standing in the house of the Lord cursing.

"So who else knows about this besides Moni?" I asked.

"No one" she said above a whisper.

"Good, you better keep that way too! Look, I don't know what you thought was gonna happen when you opened your legs to your pastor, my husband. What you thought that he would eventually leave me for you? Little girl please!" I laughed cutting her down. "That's not the way this works. What you're gonna do is take some money I give you, make an appointment at the clinic, go prop your legs on the table and have that bastard sucked out of your ass. Then you're going to stay away from my husband or I will drag yo lil ass through hell! You got that?" I said as I stepped closer in her face.

She was now shaking as she nodded her head up and down. I stared at her a couple of seconds more before I left out of the bathroom. I opened the door to find Moni standing there looking just as scared as Tish. I marched past her ass as well as I headed to my own office I had at the church. I had to gather myself together before I headed back out there to face the folks that were still in the church.

I knew Paul fucked around, but this one here was a low blow and with a damn child! There was no way in hell she was about to have my husband's child! When I went back out front, Tish, Moni and the rest of the folks were gathering their things getting ready to leave.

"Uh Tish and Moni, you can call your parents and let them know I'll be dropping you girls off home" I said politely to them.

When I made sure everything was locked up, I went outside to find the girls both waiting for me. I didn't say a word as I walked past them to my car with them following behind me. They both got in and I pulled off.

"I'm swinging by the bank to get you some money to handle you lil problem Tish, and remember what I said" I warned her as I cut my eyes over at her in the passenger seat.

"Yes ma'am" She responded.

I pulled into the bank and went inside. I made a withdrawal from my own separate account that Paul knew nothing about for the amount of $5,000. I knew that was way more than enough money, but I really wanted to make sure Tish kept her damn mouth shut. I went back to the car and handed the envelope to her full of cash.

You could tell she never saw that much money before because her eyes got big at the amount. I drove them to Tish's house and warned her ass one more time before they got out of the car and left. I never let Paul know that I knew of his involvement with Tish. After that she stopped showing up to church and then her mother mentioned how she moved to Washington after graduation with her aunt to attend school there.

I was glad that lil problem was solved, but believe me when I say that definitely wasn't the last that I had to deal with! So ever since that little ordeal with Tish, I have been distancing myself more and more from being active with the group. I would just observe things from the background. My thoughts were interrupted when my phone went off indicating I had a message.

I quickly grabbed at it hoping that it was Travis' ass finally responding to me, but was disappointed when I saw that it Paul telling me that he was going to be late coming home tonight. *What else is knew* I said out loud as I erased the message and tossed my phone back on the bed. I went into my closet and changed into my Donna Karan pants suit with matching pumps.

My hair was still fresh from my salon visit earlier. I applied some light makeup of mascara and lip gloss, sprayed on some of my Chanel #7 and headed downstairs out the door. I really didn't feel like going to this damn meeting, so I planned to be in and out. When I pulled up to the church, I saw that the ladies were all there. I walked inside to find everyone sitting and talking among themselves. As I approached the ladies, I saw Travis' daughter Candice sitting there amongst them.

"Hi Candice, I didn't expect you to be here" I said sounding surprised.

"Hello First Lady Karla. I figured that I would just stop by and see if you ladies needed any help with any events you have coming up" she said smiling.

"Oh that's thoughtful of you. Thank you for that" I said displaying a phony ass smile.

Candice has always rubbed me the wrong way. She was a spoiled ass little girl who thought that she didn't have to work for a damn thing just because Travis spoiled her ass. She also always seemed to be throwing shade my way thinking I wouldn't catch it from time to time. I really didn't know what her problem was with, nor did I care.

I sat there tuning them out as they discussed upcoming events and other bullshit as I thought about Travis. I was tired of playing this waiting game with his ass! It's been a minute now since I had some of his dick and I needed my fix!

I pulled my phone out and sent him a text telling his ass that I would be at the condo in the next hour, and that if he wasn't there I was coming to his house to get his ass! Travis knew I was crazy, and I might just be that damn crazy when it came to him. I knew he wasn't going to call my bluff though, but I still pulled his card.

Seconds later I finally got a reply back from him saying okay. Immediately I started smiling. I crossed my legs extra tight because my pussy started pulsating at the thought of Travis being inside it.

"You look mighty happy over there first lady" I

looked up to the sound of Candice's voice and to see her smirking at me.

"Oh I'm sorry ladies. It seems like the Pastor needs me home for something so I'm going to have to leave out a little early. You guys can wrap this meeting up and we'll meet again next month" I said as I stood up, gathered my things, and turned to leave.

I could have sworn I saw Candice roll her eyes at me. I swear if I wasn't fucking her daddy I would slap that bitch, but I had bigger and better things to worry about and jump on.

FATIMA

It had been two **years** since I've been back to work and it feels like I haven't missed a beat! I was so glad to get back into the swing of things that I haven't been giving Travis or his sneakiness any thought. He was back to coming home late and running to the shower so I wouldn't smell the scent of the latest perfume from whoever he was fucking.

I had been picking up as many shifts as I could and was too tired from that to even care. I still was trying to figure out a plan to get out of this disastrous marriage I was in, so in the meantime I was just working and stacking my money in a secret account Travis had no clue about. I was at home laying on the couch, I had just came home from working a twelve hour shift and I was beyond exhausted!

Travis wasn't home, which was fine with me. I didn't feel like seeing his lying ass face anyway. I dragged myself upstairs where I quickly jumped in the shower and hit the bed.

I don't know how long I was asleep, but I was awaken by fumbling sounds in my bedroom. I rolled over and cut my lamp on my nightstand on to find Travis in our walk in closet trying to remove his clothes.

"Where the hell have you been!" I asked as I jumped out the bed heading towards the closet.

"I had some things to take care of at the job" he lied boldly to my face.

"You a damn lie and you know it Travis!" I yelled in his face as I snatched at his shirt.

I was so tired of the blatant disrespect from him! It's not what you do, but how you do it and Travis just really didn't give a fuck at all anymore!

"Fatima I told you 'bout putting yo hands on me, one day I'm a put mines back on yo ass!" he threatened as he pulled away from me.

"I wish you would! And if you were so called at work, then why in the hell do you smell like you have been drowned in perfume that I don't even wear?" I busted his ass.

I assume that's why he was trying to hurry up and change out of his clothes. I'm pretty sure the bitch he was with made sure to leave her trace on him.

"I don't know what you're talking about" he answered nonchalantly as he brushed past me and headed into the bathroom.

As he tried to close the door, I blocked it with my foot and slammed it back open hoping to hit his ass in the face.

"Fatima I don't have time for this. I'm tired and I just want to take a shower and get some sleep." Travis sighed as he backed farther into the bathroom stood and by the sink.

"Oh you don't have time for this, but you think it's ok for you to be out doing God knows what with who, and then have the nerve to come home and smell like her, take a shower and go to sleep? Travis, I know it may seem like I'm a fool for you and this marriage, but I'm far from being a fool on life. I just don't understand for the life of my why you just don't give me a divorce and go on about your business, I swear you can have all of this and I won't ask for a thing" I pleaded.

At this point, I wanted nothing more than my freedom.

"I told yo ass that we ain't getting no divorce and that's that! So I suggest you stop bringing that shit up Fatima!"

"Fuck you Travis, just let me go!" I yelled.

Next thing I knew he charged towards me so fast that I didn't have time to react. He grabbed me by my neck and pinned me up against the bathroom wall.

"Now if you think I'm playing, try me and I swear if you ever try to leave me you'll be somewhere stankin'." Travis seethed through his teeth with a tight grip still around my neck.

I tried to pry his hands from around my neck, but I couldn't match his strength. After a few more seconds, he finally released his grip. I slipped down the wall grasping for air as the tears rolled my neck. Travis just stood over me breathing hard starring down at me with a look that I had never seen before. I was so terrified that I just continued to sit on the floor and not move.

"Now that we finally have that understanding, I don't want to hear another damn word about the shit" Travis finally spoke as he stared at me pure, evilness in his eyes.

I scrambled from the floor and went into the bedroom. Travis slammed the bathroom door and then I heard the shower come on. I got back into the bed crying harder, but silently as I tried to digest what the hell just happened.

CANDICE

Ever since Paul started shooting dope with me, things between us have been on point, especially the sex! He always put it down before, but when we fucked when we were high, that shit was bananas!

"So what are your plans for today baby?" I said to Paul as I rolled from on top of him.

We had just finished having another one of our fuck sessions, and I was starting to come down from my high. Lately it seemed like I never stayed high long enough, which is why I constantly stayed trying to get my next fix.

"I have some church business I need to take care of and then I'm heading home" he mentioned as he reached over on the night table and grabbed his phone.

It had been going off since he got here and I was starting to get annoyed by it. I knew it wasn't nobody but Karla's old ass probably nagging him and asking him where he was. I was so sick and tired of that bitch, and lately I haven't been trying to hide it either when I saw her.

"Ugh, I really wish you would put that shit on silent or cut it off!" I scoffed as I got up and went into the bathroom to pee.

I cut the shower on so that I could wash up real quick, which I hoped that Paul would join me instead and it would be on! I opened the door to find him sitting up on the edge of the bed trying to talk low into the phone. I crept up behind him so that I could eavesdrop.

"I know baby, I'll be there shortly I had to handle some business first. I can't wait to feel that ass" I heard him say.

I instantly became pissed off! How the fuck can this nigga say he can't wait to feel the next bitch when he was just fucking me in every hole and angle! I cleared my throat loudly letting him know I was standing right there hearing his ass! He quickly turned around almost dropping his phone.

"I gotta go" he said and hung up his phone.

"So that's what we do Paul? What my pussy not enough for you that you have to go home and fuck your damn wife!" I yelled as I stood there still naked with my arms folded across my chest.

"Candice please don't start with your dramatics. We just had a good time together so that's all you need to worry about." He brushed me off as he headed into the bathroom.

I followed right behind his ass not ready to let this go. He hopped in the shower and began washing. Seeing the soap going down his chiseled chest, and the water glistening on his sexy ass frame caused me to get wet all over again. I just couldn't get enough of him if I tried to! I jumped in the shower behind him and grabbed his rag from his hand and started washing his back.

As I was washing his back in a circular motion, I took my free hand and reached around him to massage his dick. I felt his manhood react to my touch as he got hard. I positioned myself in front of him, got on my knees with the water beating down on me and took him whole into my mouth.

"Shit!" Paul yelled out as he leaned up against the wall.

I grabbed his dick with both hands and went to work. I was sucking and jacking him off at the same time. I deep throated Paul and that threw him overboard! Within minutes, I felt him shaking which meant he was about to cum. He gripped my hair from the top of my head and screamed out as he blessed my mouth with all his seeds.

I wasn't done there though, I made sure I got every last drop. Once I was done, I stood up and grabbed the wash rag and went back to washing him. I always made sure to do whatever it was I had to do to take care of Paul. Since I knew he had a wife, I knew that I always needed to stay on my shit!

After we were done showering, we both headed back into the room and got dressed. I decided not to bring back up the subject of what I heard. I didn't want to nag him because I'm pretty sure he already got enough of that at home.

"When am I'm going to see you again?" I asked putting on my shoes.

"Soon."

"Really Paul?" I said with an attitude.

It seemed like more and more he was starting to brush me off. Hell, before today, I hadn't seen him in two weeks! I even went to that dumb ass meeting his wife holds at the church just to see if he was gonna be there, but he wasn't. I had to play it off and act like I was there because I was interested and be around her ass. She left the meeting early that day saying she needed to get home to him.

I wanted to beat that bitch's ass right there in the House of the Lord and send her ass to meet him early, but I had to hold my composure. Instead I tried calling Paul all that evening hoping to ruin whatever it was they were doing, but he never answered my calls or texts.

"Candice you know the church revival is coming up and I need to prepare for that. We have over ten pastors this year visiting us and I need to make sure I leave an impression on them." he explained.

I knew Paul was giving me a lame ass excuse, but I just took it. As bad as I wanted to argue and let him know that it was bullshit, from the way he was acting lately I realized I needed to continue to act as the understanding woman and not give him and more grief. My ultimate goal was to get rid of Karla and I become the first lady and Paul's wife.

"I understand baby, well you know I'm here waiting on you daddy" I said seductively as I walked over to him wrapping my arms around his neck and plunging my tongue down his throat.

"That's why you're my baby girl" Paul said slapping me on my ass as we broke free.

We both said our goodbyes as we looked on cautiously and headed in our separate directions. Paul pulled off ahead of me, and something in my gut told me to follow him. I don't know why, but it was just something telling me that he wasn't heading home. I finally pulled out of the motel parking lot and trailed him. I made sure to be a couple of cars behind him so that he wouldn't notice me.

We were driving for about fifteen minutes when I noticed that he was bypassing his exit to get on the highway to go home.

I fucking knew it! I said out loud as I continued to follow. I didn't know where the fuck Paul was going, but I was about to be right on his ass finding out! I stayed a couple of cars back trailing him for about another twenty minutes. Where ever we were heading was surely out in the boondocks because this shit was way out of sight.

Finally Paul pulled into a drive way of this house back from the roads. The house was secluded and looked nice. I stayed back and parked my car down the road and decided to walk back to the house instead. I crept up slowly as I approached the house. I looked around making sure no one else could see me.

I didn't know if there was anyone else there because Paul's car was the only one in the driveway and the garage door was down. I decided to go around back and see if I could see anything in the window. Soon as I got to the back, I peeked in the window and noticed that it I was looking into the kitchen. But what I saw next made me almost piss in my pants!

Paul was sitting at the kitchen table getting his shoulders massaged and neck kissed on by Marcus! I took my phone out and made sure my flash was off my camera and the shutter was on silent and started snapping away at pictures.

Once I couldn't stand the sight of this sick shit no more, I quietly made my way back to the front of the house and back down the road to my car. I got in my car and hauled ass back to my side of the town. Hurt and angry was an understatement on how I was feeling right now! Not only did I have to deal with him having a wife, but now I'm supposed to deal with him fucking the town's transvestite too!?

Naw, fuck that! Paul had another thing coming if he thought I was about to play the third wheel, matter of fact it's about time I become the queen bitch; and I have the ammunition to do so!

PAUL

No matter how hard I tried to live by the word I teach every Sunday, Satan just seems to keep winning in my life. I find myself falling deeper and deeper into sin, because here I was laying up next to Marcus when I was just laid up with Candice earlier.

How I got here with Marcus in the first place was based on my hidden desires I had since I was a young boy. Ever since I was young, I used to always fantasize about what it would be like being with a man. Of course growing up in the south, being a homosexual would get you lynched right along with being black!

My first curiosity came when I was about twelve years old. I was playing football with some of the other boys in the field. There was this older boy name Ronnie who was on the opposite team. He wasn't from my home town and was visiting for the summer. Anyway, I got the ball and began to run when he tackled me and fell on top of me along

125

with the other dudes. Ronnie and I were on the bottom of the pile and I swear I felt someone touching me on my dick.

Once I was able to get up, I shook the thought out of my head and continued to play. Every time I had the ball, Ronnie would make it his business to tackle me and I would still feel like someone was touching my dick. After the game, I headed back to walk home when Ronnie caught up with me and asked if he could walk with me.

I didn't mind. As we were walking we started asking questions about one another. I decided to take a short cut to my house through these abandon buildings, with Ronnie still following me. Right when we walked through one building, Ronnie pushed me up against the wall and started gripping my dick.

"I know you felt me doing this earlier when we were on the ground." He breathed into my ear as he was grinding on me.

I just stood there speechless and still. I knew this was wrong, but the feelings I was feeling felt so good! Next thing I knew, Ronnie got down on his knees, pulled my dick out and started sucking on it! I had never experienced anything like this before and I felt good! I started getting into the rhythm and pumping myself in and out of Ronnie mouth until I felt some stuff oozing out of me.

That was my first time ejaculating and with another boy at that! After that experience, for the rest of the summer Ronnie and I would sneak off with one another and have sex. He taught me how to suck dick, the trick to taking it in the ass, and giving it. Every time I was with him, I felt guilty afterwards but I still couldn't stop.

I was happy when the summer came to an end and Ronnie went home because I felt like I was free from doing those sinful things again. I kept what I did a secret and hidden for years until I met with Marcus. When I ran into him in North Carolina while I was on a church conference, I knew who he was when I first saw him.

His grandmother was a loyal member of my church and would often talk with me and have prayer for him. She showed me a picture of him when he completely transformed over while in LA and ask if I would pray for him to have those demons removed from him. Even though she loved him unconditionally, she was still a praying grandmother hoping he would change his life.

So when I spotted Marcus at the hotel we were having the conference at, those feelings started emerging again. That night when I approached him and met up with him in his room, he confessed that he really was a man and that was fine with me. Marcus was a bad ass woman and the only thing that confirmed that she was a he was what was between his legs. From that day forward he's been allowing me to live my other life.

He desired to have his dick removed, but I was against it. I didn't have to say it, but Marcus knew I enjoyed having the best of both worlds with him. I was shocked when he decided to move back with his grandmother though. I knew she was ill, but I thought that he would take care of her from LA and visit occasionally. When I saw him that Sunday in church, I almost choked in the pulpit.

Later on that evening, we met up and he confirmed that he was only here to see about his grandmother and nothing more. Then he started hanging with Karla and I was sure he had a motive then! Time went on and no one still didn't know about my other life and Marcus and I still continued to do our thing without anyone knowing.

I admit, it was beginning to be hard work trying to maintain my wife, Candice and Marcus. I had to stay on top of the lies I was constantly having to tell to Karla and Candice. Marcus was the only one that I didn't have to lie to and be myself around. If this was another world and time, I would be with him and only him, but I can't.

"Why are you laying over there so quiet?" Marcus asked breaking me out of my thoughts.

"I'm just thinking what life would be like if it was just me and you" I confessed.

"Well it's not that hard to find out."

"Marcus you know we can't be together like that" I reminded him.

"Paul this is 2015 and ain't nobody living in the closet like that anymore. Hell you got preachers that's out there now! You just chose to make your life difficult for you."

"Marcus we have been over this. I'm a pastor with a wife, I can't just up and hurt all the people that depend on me including my congregation." I explained.

"Paul that's bullshit and you know it! It's funny how you don't want to hurt them but willing to be miserable in the process. How long do you think you're going to be able to keep this up huh? When my grandma gets well enough to be on her own, I'm out of this slow ass town and not looking back, so I suggest you decide what it is you want to do." Marcus replied as he sat up in the bed.

The thought of him leaving caused me to panic on the inside. I was in love with him and he knew it, so I didn't want to see my life without him. I wasn't in love with Karla anymore, and Candice was a piece of ass to me. Marcus was where my heart was at and it hurt that I couldn't share that with the world. I knew that if I completely gave myself to him that I would be damned to hell.

My life was spinning so much out of control that no matter how hard I tried to grasp it, I couldn't control it.

"Paul you know you could always come with me. Shit you could be a traveling preacher and settle in LA with me" he offered.

This wasn't the first time Marcus had offered me to go back to LA with him and live freely, but I just couldn't leave Alexandria. I may have been a pastor in a small town, but my reputation was big. I refused to be in the world of scandal with leaving my wife to be with a man.

"So how is your grandmother's chemo coming along?" I asked changing the subject.

"The treatments themselves are taking their toll on her. She's so weak from them and the throwing up is draining her as well. But overall, they are working. She's a real trooper with having both of her breasts removed, hell she said she didn't have a man to suck on them anyway" Marcus laughed.

I joined him picturing her saying that.

"Well that's a blessing. She's a fighter and God is surely not ready for her yet."

"Paul can you not start that preaching shit. I'm not up

for hearing that" Marcus complained rolling his eyes.

"I'm going to get something to drink, you want anything?" he offered.

"Yea, bring me back some water please."

Marcus got up from the bed naked and glistening, and walked out of the room into the kitchen. I heard my phone beeping. I reached for it off the night stand and saw that I had a text message. I opened to see that it was from Candice. It indicated that I had a picture message, I downloaded it and when it came into view I jumped out the bed.

"What the fuck!" I screamed out loud.

"What is it?" Marcus said as he came back into the room with two water bottles.

I stood there speechless as I starred at my phone. Marcus came over to me to see what it was I was looking at.

"Oh my God!" he said with his hand over his mouth.

We both stood there in shock as Candice sent me a picture of Marcus kissing all over my neck and with a message saying *I guess my pussy isn't enough huh.*

TRAVIS

I never in my life put my hands on a woman before I choked up Fatima the other night. I honestly didn't mean to, but I was already pissed off from the stunt Karla pulled earlier that day with threatening to come to my home if I didn't fuck her that day; and Fatima singing that divorce shit in my ear when I got home later on that night just took me over the edge. I may do what I do, but I'm not letting her ass go!

Fatima is a good woman, and I'd be damn if I allow another man to reap those benefits. She's been giving me the silent treatment since that day, but that's to be expected. I needed to find a way to be done with Karla's ass though. I don't take to kindly to threats and she just showed how far she would go by doing that.

I knew that if I tried to break things off with her now, that she would become a problem. When we first started fucking around, I thought that this was one affair that could be kept under wraps with no complications from the both of us. I mean, she had just as much to lose than I did! But just like any other mistress, she started catching main woman feelings and now she on some type of demand shit and I wasn't having it!

I was on my way to the church for our monthly Deacon Board meeting. Tonight I was presenting the drawings Paul and I chose for the design of the new church. It would also be the cheapest, but they wouldn't know that part. Paul and I came to the agreement to let them think that this would be right where our budget was and skim off the top of the money. That way, we both will walk away with $15,000 apiece.

I pulled up to the church to see that the rest of the deacons and the pastor were already there. I walked inside and greeted everyone and got down to business.

"Okay gentleman, this is the design the Pastor and I agreed upon on. It has all the necessities and space that we all agreed on and it's right there on the head with our budget." I explained as I pointing at the designs on the projection.

I got the confirmation that they were on board by the nodding of their heads in agreement. We spent another thirty minutes going over the numbers and setting a date to begin breaking ground. All through the meeting, I noticed how quiet Paul was. Normally he would be the one leading the meetings, but he just sat there like the rest and let me handle everything. After every one was satisfied, we ended the meeting in prayer and left.

"Pastor, can I speak to you for a moment?" I asked Paul as he was leaving out of the room.

"Sure" he said as he stopped and came back to take a seat.

Once every one left the room, I closed the door and took a seat across from him.

"What's going on Paul, because you were exceptionally quiet throughout the whole meeting" I inquired.

"Man I just got so much stuff going on at home. I'm sorry about that."

"Naw, it's cool. Is there anything I can do to help?" I offered.

Whatever Karla was doing was really stressing him out because I have never seen him like this.

"This is something I have to handle on my own, but thanks for the offer" he replied.

"Alright, well call me if you need me" I said as I got up and gave him a pat on the shoulder as I headed out of the room.

I left out of the church and headed into the parking lot where I got into my car and headed home. I knew Fatima would still be there getting ready to go to work. She started working the night shift lately which I know it was just to avoid being home with me.

I hated that we were on these terms, but I just needed some time to figure out how I was going to handle this Karla situation and make things right with my wife. When I pulled up home, Fatima's car was still in the driveway. I walked inside to an empty living room.

I walked up the stairs to find her in the bedroom with her matching bra and panties changing into her scrubs. Her body was so fucking beautiful and toned. My dick started jumping in my pants hoping to feel the inside of her, but I already knew she wasn't about to give me no ass.

"Hey baby" I greeted her.

"Hey" she answered back dryly as she was moving around the room avoiding me at all costs.

"Fatima can we talk?" I asked taking a seat on the edge of the bed.

"I have to get ready for work."

"I know but it won't take long" I pleaded grabbing her hand lightly as she passed me.

She stopped and turned around looking at me as if she

really didn't want to hear anything I had to say.

"Look baby, I'm so sorry about putting my hands on you the other day. I promise I will never do anything like that again! I just didn't know how to control my feelings when you told me that you wanted a divorce. Fatima, I love you more than life itself and the thought of being without you tears me up baby!" I said with sincerity looking her in her eyes hoping she believed me.

She just stared at me for a few seconds. She finally removed my hand from hers and told me that she had to go, when she went into the bathroom to continue to get dressed. I got up and went back downstairs to fix me a quick sandwich. Moments later Fatima came down, grabbed her purse and keys and left out the door without so much as a goodbye.

I fixed my sandwich and sat at the island eating. The house was quiet, but my thoughts were loud as hell. I knew my wife deserved better, but I refused to let her have that with someone else. I knew that I could be the man she needed me to be again, but this thing with Karla was too deep. This bitch acted as if she didn't care if Paul found out she was fucking around.

When I met her at the condo that day she text me, I tried talking some sense into her ass and let her know that we needed to cool it, but she wasn't trying to hear me. She told me that she wanted what she wanted and that was me. Right there I knew she was becoming obsessed with what we were doing.

I fucked her with no emotion and tried to unleash as much pain on her as I could, but it seemed like the harder I went the more she enjoyed that shit! Normally I would be passionate with her, but this time I wouldn't even kiss her! Every time she tried to kiss me I would turn my head. Then I just told her to turn over on her stomach and fucked her from the back altogether so I wouldn't have to look at her ass.

Afterwards, I tried to reason with her again by telling her that we needed to chill, but that's when she told me that if I thought of leaving her, that she would bring us both down by telling everyone that we had been having an affair. I couldn't believe this bitch had the nerve to go there knowing damn well what could happen.

I wished like hell I had never fucked with her ass, but it's too late for that now. I left there that day and have been dodging her calls again, but I knew I would have to answer her sooner than later. I continued to sit there and eat my food when my phone rang. I noticed that it was an unknown number. I never answer unknown calls, but something told me to answer this one.

"Hello?"

"I have a way to get rid of that bitch Karla, and I think we both could benefit from it" the caller on the other end of the phone spoke.

"Who is this?" I asked confused.

"You'll find out soon enough, I'll text you an address and I want you to meet me there a week from today at 6pm. Don't be late, and don't say shit to anyone about this either. I'll see you tomorrow, if you decide not to show just know that bitch will try and make your life a living hell." And with that the caller hung up.

The voice came from a woman, but I couldn't recognize it. The call ended and next thing I knew I received a text with an address. It must have come from a burner phone because it still didn't show a number. I don't know what the hell was going on, but I damn sure was about to find out.

FATIMA

I was beyond tired, but right now I felt like I had no choice but to work as much as I could so that I wouldn't have to be home. I also wanted to stack as much money as I could so I could get the fuck away from Travis and this damn town! I knew that if I told my folks what was going on that they would help me and want me to come back home, but I didn't leave there in the first place just to go back.

I was starting to have a pattern of no matter where I went, bad luck would follow me. I was still in shock from what Paul did to me the other night. I would have never thought that he would put his hands on me! I was so scared of the look in his eyes, that I thought that he was actually going to hurt me. For the first time, I was afraid of him which was why I was trying to avoid him. Even when he called himself apologizing, I still wasn't trying to hear that shit.

I wanted nothing more than to spit in his fucking face, but I knew if I would have done that, he probably would have knocked my teeth out. So I just left out the house without saying a word to him. It was Friday night, and the ER had been busy nonstop! I don't know what was in the air, but it seem like we were getting these young ass kids coming in all night long for doing some shit. I recognized most of them, and when they saw me they quickly put their heads down trying to avoid eye contact.

Finally I was able to catch a breather once the rush slowed down. I was standing against the counter with my head in my hands trying to get myself together.

"You okay" I looked up to see Tonya standing next to me.

"Yeah girl, I'm just tired that's all." I said as I stood straight up and stretched.

"Well you have been working nonstop since you've been back. I mean I'm glad that you're back, but I don't want you to burn yourself out." Tonya said with concern.

"I know, I just don't want to be home as much that's all" I sighed shaking my head.

I didn't tell Tonya that Travis had put his hands on me, because I was ashamed. She already knew I was putting up with his lies and cheating, I didn't want her to know that I was now also putting up with his hands.

"Look, why don't you move in with me? I keep

telling you that you don't have to keep putting up with Travis' shit Fatima" she expressed.

I continued to stand there for a moment quiet, contemplating her offer. I wanted nothing more than to leave this bullshit ass marriage and haul ass, but I didn't want to put her in the middle of my mess. I also knew that **Travis** would probably act a fool if he knew that I left to go stay with her.

"I really appreciate the offer Hun, but this is something I have to deal with on my own".

"I know you can deal with it on your own Fatima, but you don't have to! I could tell that you are beyond tired of what's going on. I see it in your face every time we are around one another. And add on the fact that you are taking on all these double shifts confirm it, just let me be here for you."

"You are here for me, by being the great friend you are, being my shoulder to lean on and my ear when I need to vent. You truly are my best friend Tonya, but I really need to handle this on my own. Trust me when I say I'm working on a plan to be rid of all of this" I informed her as I gave her a hug.

"Alright, well whatever it is that you got cooking up, just make sure you put ya girl on. I wanna kick some ass too!" Tonya laughed.

I joined in on her crazy ass knowing she was serious.

"Listen, since we both are about to get off and don't have to work for the next three days, why don't we hit the spot that we went to a couple of weeks back? We both could use some drinks and truthfully, the last time we were there it was some fine men walking around there! I'm in a drought, so I'm on the prowl for some new dick!" Tonya said laughing looking around to make sure no one else heard her.

I don't know about the place crawling with good looking men the last time we were there, because I was just having a good time with good music and drinks. Although I know Travis stay doing him, I'm not the type of woman to cheat on the person I'm with. Considering that I liked the atmosphere from the last time and didn't want to go home to a begging ass man who full of *I'm sorry's,* I decided to take Tonya up on her offer.

"Alright girl, I'm down!" I told her.

"Good, meet me at my house around nine and we can leave from there" Tonya instructed.

The rest of the day went by smooth. I received occasional texts form Travis telling me that he loves me and how sorry he is. I erased those shits just as quick as they came to my phone. Soon as I was about to get off, he sent a message telling me that he was about to head out for a couple of hours, normally I would question where he was going, but this time I made it my business this time to just reply back saying okay.

I felt some type of relief knowing he wasn't going to be home when I got there. Once I was off, I hurried home so that I could soak in my Jacuzzi tub before I left for the club. After I took my bath, I decided on wearing a turquoise body con dress with my black suede Manalo pumps, and my black half jacket. I unwrapped my hair and combed it down with a part in the middle.

I had just recently added some blond highlights to it, so it was fierce! I applied some mascara on my long lashes that were often mistaken for fake ones, and nude color Revlon lipstick on my lips. I gave myself a once over in my full-lenth mirror and loved what I saw! No one would ever guess that I was a deacon's wife.

I sprayed on my Burberry Brit, grabbed my clutch and headed downstairs to head over to Tonya. I was excited to be actually be going out again tonight, it helped me keep my mind occupied from what I was dealing with at home. But I had a gut feeling that tonight was really about to be off the hook!

CANDICE

I just spent the last thirty minutes in my apartment getting high. After I sent Paul the text of him and Marcus' punk ass, he's been blowing my phone up! If only he would be calling me under different circumstances than that, but I already knew what it was about. I knew I had his ass under my control now, I just needed some time to decide what it was I wanted to do with him.

I loved Paul and was definitely in love with him, but I was also pissed and hurt at the fact that he was fucking dick and pussy! I should have felt more disgusted than betrayed, but I didn't. What I wanted was for him to be mines and all mines by any cost! Once again my phone started ringing, I looked at it and saw that it was my daddy calling.

I haven't spoken to him in a while and I knew that if I didn't answer he would be knocking at my door. I didn't want him to see me high, so I answered.

"Hi daddy." I answered trying not to sound sluggish.

"Hi baby girl, I was calling to check on you since I haven't heard from you in a while" he spoke.

"Well I did come by your house a couple of weeks ago, but you're stuck up wife told me you weren't there and slammed the door in my face" I explained telling the semi-truth.

"Fatima never mentioned you coming by" He said completely ignoring what I said about her slamming the door in my face.

"I'm sure she didn't." I said sarcastically.

"So what have you been up, have you been looking for a job?" he questioned.

I sucked my teeth out loud showing my annoyance. I knew that was the real reason why he was calling, just so he can be all in my damn business.

"I've been looking, but ain't nobody hiring." I lied.

I haven't been looking for shit. Why the hell do I need to really work when my daddy was making cash and not to mention the big payout I could possibly have coming up from Paul.

"Well baby girl, you need to get on your grind because I can't keep supporting you all your life. That was the main reason I paid for your college education, so you would be able to take care of yourself."

I pulled the phone from my ear and looked up at the ceiling as I heard him reciting the same damn speech he always says every time he mentions me having a job. He really was trying to blow my damn high, and I wasn't having it!

"Dad look, I said I'm trying okay? Besides, I'm sure your wife must be in your ear telling you that I need a job" I interrupted.

"Fatima has nothing to do with this, so stop trying to make this about her. This is about you being a grown woman who has her daddy supporting her. I refuse to keep paying your rent, utilities, car note and insurance. Not to mention making sure you have money in your account! You need to get your life together and quick Candice!"

"I gotta go dad, I'll talk to you later" I said and hung up the phone abruptly.

The main thing I didn't want him to do he did, and that was blow my fucking high! I reached over to my nightstand to grab my dope only to see I was running short. I would only have enough for one shoot up and then I would have to re cop. I already knew the money I currently had in my account was just enough for me to have gas and food until my dad deposited more.

By the way he was sounding, hell he might not even

do that!

I knew that I definitely needed to get on my shit now, and I knew just how I was gonna do that. I reached back for my phone and sent Paul a text telling him to meet me at my place tonight. He quickly replied back saying he would be here in an hour. Good, that gave me time to get myself together.

PAUL

I was finally relieved when I received a text from Candice telling her to meet me at her place tonight. Ever since she sent me those texts of Marcus and me, I had been trying my hardest to talk to her. I wanted to know how the hell she even knew about us! I had so many questions, but she was ignoring me. I was on my way over to her place now, in hopes that I could talk some sense into her and make sure my secret stays just that!

I was driving fast as normal. I reached her apartment in about fifteen minutes nervous as hell. I wouldn't normally come over to her place because of the fear of someone might seeing me, that's why we would meet up somewhere else. But this time, I had to come here on her terms.

I parked as far away from her building as I could, got out looking around making sure I was unnoticed and headed to her door. Candice lived in some nice apartments which I already knew Travis was paying for. I nervously knocked on her door and seconds later she answered the door in some boy shorts and a sports bra.

I walked straight in without speaking and went to take a seat on the couch. My hands were sweating and my heart was beating so loud that I thought you could hear it out of my chest.

"You want something to drink?" Candice offered as she came into the living room.

"No I'm fine" I said clearing my throat.

"Well I guess we already know why you're here. So when did you start liking dick?" she asked standing in from of me with her arms folded across her chest.

I sat back on the couch and tried to get myself comfortable before talking.

"I don't know what you think you saw, but it wasn't even like that" I mustered up. I knew it sounded cliché, but that was the only thing I could come up with.

Candice started laughing as she went and took a seat across from me on the sofa chair.

"Negro please! The eyes don't lie and neither do pictures! I know what the fuck I saw and that was you getting a massage by a fucking punk and then him kissing you on your neck! I mean damn, I already knew I would have to compete with a wife, but now I have to compete with a dude too?" Candice said loudly.

"I really wish you would lower your voice, and like I said, it's not what you think" I calmly said.

"Then explain it to me then Paul."

I sat there for a few moments quiet contemplating on what it was I was about to say. I already knew I was busted, but still couldn't bring myself to admitting anything!

"Look, whatever else I have going on doesn't affect you and I. You will always be my baby and no one can take your place" I tried my best to sound as genuine as possible.

"That's bullshit and you know it Paul. But you know what's so hilarious about all of this; I know you better than your wife and your dude! I know that not only do you shoot dope, but that you're also a damn faggot!"

"I'm not a faggot!" I clenched through my teeth trying to control my anger. This bitch was really pissing me off!

"Oh so you like getting fucked up the ass then?" she laughed.

I found myself getting more pissed by the second. I scooted to the edge of the couch and folded my hands together. I had to gain my composure back and try to reason with this bitch. I already knew what Candice was on and she was about to make this hard for me.

"What is it that you want Candice?" I finally asked.

"What I want is for you to make sure I want for nothing."

"What do you mean by that?" I asked confused.

"First off, you need to make sure $10,000 is deposited into my account every month."

"$10,000 are you out of your mind! How am I supposed to do that without it being unnoticed from my wife!" I was now the loud one.

"That's your problem, not mines to figure out. I also want you to be available to give me that good dick whenever I call for it! No more fucking me on your terms Paul."

I couldn't believe the shit that was coming out of her mouth. I expected her to be pissed about me and Marcus and be crying all over the place. Instead she's sitting her junky ass over there trying to blackmail me! The more I look at her, the more I see a woman I wish I never stuck my dick in.

"Let's be reasonable here Candice. There's no way I can give you that much money monthly without Karla noticing it. And if I do and she realizes it, we'll both be busted" I explained.

"You think I give a fuck about people, especially her finding out about me and you? To answer your question fuck no! I could care less Paul. All I know is I better have my ten grand in my account every month or the whole damn town and beyond will know that the good Reverend Paul Stanley likes to suck dick" she threatened.

I must have blacked out because next thing I know, I jumped from where I was sitting and standing over Candice chocking the shit out of her! I was squeezing her neck so hard that her eyes were bulging out of her head as she was trying to pry my hands away from her neck. I knew my strength was beyond hers and the next thing I heard was a crack and her head going limp.

I stepped back snapping out of my trance to see that I had indeed broke Candice's neck and killed her. I started wiping down my hands on the side of my pants as if I could wash away my prints away.

I was sweating so profusely that I ran into the kitchen and splashed some water on my face. I looked back into the living room to see Candice lying lifeless in the chair. I cut her lights off and went to the front door to leave. I looked out cautiously making sure no one saw me leaving, and walked back to my car.

Good thing I parked far away from her building, that way if somebody does see me, they wouldn't know where I was coming from. Once I made it to my car, I jumped in and pulled off. I kept looking in my rearview mirror making sure no one was behind me. I sighed a sigh of relief when I reached my exit to get on the expressway to head home.

Heavenly father I ask that you forgive me for this sin I just committed. I said out loud as I headed back home.

FATIMA

I did something I have never done the night Tonya and I went out to the club for drinks, I gave another man my phone number. His name is Quincy and we've been texting ever since. That night we got to the club, I did take notice to the fine men flowing through there. Although I had no plans of touching, I damn sure wasn't depriving myself of looking.

Tonya and I were turning heads the moment we walked through the door. I was dressed sexy yet classy, while Tonya didn't leave anything to the imagination with a sheer all over body suit that looked like it was painted on her body. I must admit, my girl was bad and I wish I had the courage to wear that, but I was fine and comfortable on with what I had on.

Anyway, we found a table and ordered our first round of drinks. I would only have two max while Tonya splurged. I knew I would be the designated driver, so I kept it light. I just wanted to drink enough to keep me mellow and my mind off of my home life. After sitting at our table for about thirty minutes, Ashanti feat. Beanie Man *First Real Love* started blasting through the speakers.

"Oh girl that's my song!" I yelled as I jumped and grabbed Tonya's hand and led her to the dance floor.

I don't know what came over me, but I started winding my ass to the reggae mix beat as if I was the only one on the dance floor. By now I had taken off my jacket and was displaying all of my curves. I was so in tune with the song that next thing I knew I felt a pair of soft hands grabbing my waist from behind. I quickly turned around to see who was touching me. I was greeted by the most handsome face I ever laid eyes on!

"Excuse you?" I said as I gently removed his hands from my hips and backed up a little bit to put space between us.

"I'm sorry, but when I saw you over here dancing like that and these group of vultures started surrounding you, I felt like I had to come over here and protect what's mines" he said showing this sexy ass grin.

Oh my God, this man had a set of deep dimples and perfect teeth! I had to quickly gather myself because I was starring hard at him and I didn't want him to notice.

"Well I'm not yours, but I appreciate the concern" I

said calmly as I walked off back to our table.

When I made it back there, I noticed that Tonya's ass was still on the dance floor with some dude looking like they were about to fuck any minute with the way they were dancing. The waitress came back over and I ordered us some waters so I could cool down. As soon as she came back with our waters, I guzzled mines down.

I looked back on the dance floor and noticed that I didn't see Mr. handsome anywhere. I don't even know why I was looking for this man, but I was. I decided to just sit for a while and relax. My feet were starting to bother me from all the dancing I had done earlier, so I took my shoes off and started rubbing my right foot.

"Let me take care of that for you" I heard the same sexy baritone voice from earlier say.

I looked up to see him again, this time standing in front of me and in a better light view. I swear the light did this man no justice! He was even finer now than in the dark!

"What, are you stalking me?" I asked laughing.

He didn't say anything. He just flashed that smile again while he took a seat next to me. He then grabbed ahold of both of my feet and put them in his lap and started massaging them. It took everything in me not to lean my head back, close my eyes, and let out a moan! This man's hands felt so damn good and soft on my body as if they were made for it!

"You can go ahead and let out a moan, I know it feels good" he boasted.

So far I gathered that he was either that damn cocky or just confident. Either way it was turning me on and that wasn't supposed to happen! Even though I didn't really want to, I reluctantly removed my feet from his lap and put my shoes back on. He started laughing as he watched me.

"What's your name Ms. Lady?" he asked me.

The music was so loud, but it was as if we were the only ones in the room and that I could only hear him.

"My name is Fatima." I responded.

"Well it's nice to meet you Fatima, I'm Quincy." He extended his hand for me to shake.

I put my small hands in the palm of his and shook it.

"Look, I didn't mean any disrespect from earlier. It's just I saw you when you walked in with your friend from earlier and believe me when I say, you stuck out and I mean that in a good way" he complemented.

I couldn't help but blush. I knew I had no business sitting here and even talking to this man or thinking the thoughts I was thinking since I was still a married woman, but it was like an instant attraction and I was being drawn to him.

"Thank you, and that's okay" I mustered.

I started getting really nervous and began to look around the club as if I was looking for someone. I was mainly trying to avoid eyes contact with him.

"Are you looking for someone?" he questioned.

"Uh yes, my girlfriend I came here with" I answered nervously.

"Looks like she's having a good time to me." He pointed on the dance floor laughing.

The song had changed to a slow jam, and Tonya and the same dude I saw her dancing with earlier were now grinding with one another still dancing. I couldn't help but laugh also, because if I knew her I knew that her drought would be over soon!

"So you're married?" Quincy asked pointing his eyes at my finger.

"With a rock like that, it's hard to miss" he said as he circled my diamond with the tip of his finger.

I moved my hand back as I spoke. "Yes I'm married."

"Well congratulations, marriage is a beautiful thing."

"Are you married?" I asked even though I didn't see a ring on his finger.

"If I was, I wouldn't be here let alone talking to you."

It was something about the way he said that, that caused my kitty to pulsate. I had to cross my legs tight in hoping I could calm down.

"So what are you having, a girls night out?" Quincy asked.

"Yes, but it seems like my girlfriend might have found her a new friend." I laughed as I saw Tonya and old boy heading in the direction of the bathrooms.

"Well it's nothing wrong with meeting new people and having friends." He flirted.

I knew where he was getting at with this, and although I had a lying, piece of shit husband at home, it just wasn't in me to do what he was doing.

"You're right about that Mr. Quincy, but in my place I'm fine on the new friends tip. It was really nice meeting you and thank you for the mini foot massage, but I have to find my girl and get going." I quickly jumped up and grabbed my things and headed into the direction of the bathrooms. There was no line or anything, so I walked in.

Soon as I opened the door, Tonya was standing at the mirror fixing herself and the guy she was with was just about to walk out. He looked at me and grinned in passing.

"I guess your drought is finally over huh?" I asked shaking my head.

"Hell no, it was a damn waist of a nut. His ass couldn't fuck to save his life." She responded reapplying her lipstick.

I just shook my head laughing as we both left of the restroom and headed outside the club. On the drive back over to our side of town, we were replaying tonight events. Tonya had me cracking up when she was telling me how the dude she went in the bathroom for a quickie with, was doing all that damn moaning and breaking a sweat before he even got it in!

"Girl you are crazy!" I hollered laughing.

"Um huh, but anyways I saw you talking to that tall, fine ass caramel brotha! Girl I thought you was gonna take his ass in the bathroom and have a little fun of your own!" she exclaimed.

"Child please, you know I'm not on that. Besides I'm still a married woman Tonya" I reminded.

"Girl what good is a marriage when only one of your asses are honoring your vows? I say go out and have you some damn fun. You don't have to fuck another man to have fun Fatima."

I didn't say anything else as I continued to drive. Tonya was busy texting on her phone so she was quiet as well. When we finally got back to her house, she asked me if

I wanted to just spend the night there so I wouldn't have to go home and deal with Travis; but I declined her offer and headed on home. Travis wasn't there when I left and I hope his ass wasn't there when I got home.

My mind kept drifting back to Quincy. I had no business thinking about this man, but I just couldn't help it. The way he smiled and the way his dimples set so deep in his cheeks kept flashing in my mind. The soft touch of his hands on my waist when I was dancing, then the touch of his hands massaging my feet. I started to get moist between my legs just reminiscing on it!

Twenty minutes later I pulled up home and noticed that Travis still wasn't home. It was now 2am, and normally I would be blowing up his phone to see where he was at but right now I could care less. I went inside and headed straight to the shower so I could wash the club scene off of me. I cut the shower on and stripped naked out of my clothes.

I looked myself over in the mirror and noticed how beautiful I was on the outside, but felt so ugly and frail on the inside. I put my shower cap on and stepped inside the shower and let the hot water beat down on me.

I grabbed my loofa where I poured my Hawaiian Tahitian body wash and started washing my body slowly. The loofa felt so soft against my skin, that I closed my eyes and pictured that it was Quincy's hands instead. I found myself traveling farther down to my honey pot and rubbing on my clit in a circular motion. I started moaning softly and rotating my hips as I was grinding on my loofa. Moment later I felt myself cumming and released all of my juices.

I opened my eyes with heavy breathing, and continued to wash myself clean. Soon as I got out the shower I was exhausted, so I put on my night shirt and jumped into my bed tired and satisfied! I closed my eyes and drifted off to sleep, only to be awoken by the sound of my cell phone vibrating on the night stand. I reached over and saw an unfamiliar number texting me.

Message: I hope you made it home Ms. Lady. I instantly got butterflies in my stomach. I already knew who it was, question was how the hell he got my number! I had to play it off cool though.

Me: Um who is this?

Him: I'm pretty sure you know who this is, besides I highly doubt there is somebody else calling you Ms. Lady.

Me: how did you get my number?

Him: your home girl gave it to me when you left the dance floor.

I thought back to after I finished dancing, I looked for him on the floor and didn't see him. That damn Tonya always trying to be sneaky! Her ass will be hearing from me about giving my number out, but deep down I was glad she did.

Me: well I'll have to talk to her about that, but I did get home safe and it's late.

Him: that's all I wanted to hear, you getting home safe. I'm going to let you go to sleep with the hopes of you dreaming about me so I'll text you later on-good night beautiful.

Me: lol good night Mr. Conceited.

Ever since that night, Quincy and I have been texting and talking on the phone every day. I learned that he's thirty one, no kids and a real estate agent who owned his own company. He said that he was traveling to Alexandria to see if there was any potential property there for him to profit on. He was single and not really looking for a relationship right now which I liked.

I'm glad he wasn't looking for more than I could offer him, so we both just enjoyed having conversation. I was open about me and my situation. When I told him that my husband was a deacon he spent the last five minutes laughing in my damn ear. He couldn't believe that I was the wife of a deacon.

Speaking of deacon, things between Travis and I have

been getting more strained by the day. I make sure to work on Sunday's so I wouldn't have to go to that so called place of a church, and I'm also still working the night shift so that I wouldn't have to see him at home as much. Besides, that gives me more time to talk to Quincy and not have to worry about Travis finding out.

I admit, ever since I have been talking to Quincy, he has kept my mind occupied from what is going on at home. Travis was still coming and going when he pleased with no questions from me, and I was still planning on leaving his ass and this marriage real soon.

TRAVIS

I don't know what's been going on lately, but Fatima seems like she's distancing herself more and more from me. It's like we are damn roommates in this house! When I'm working during the day she's home, when I come home during the night she's getting ready to go to work. She only talks to me if I speak to her first and her answers are always short.

She stopped coming to church and just seems like she is living a separate life all of a sudden. It's almost like I can do whatever I want and come and go as I please and she doesn't have a care in the world. Hell, I can't even remember the last time my wife even text or called my phone without me reaching out to her first! The thought did cross my mind of her possibly messing around with someone else, but I quickly dismissed that thought because I knew Fatima wasn't that kind of woman. I was still avoiding Karla at all costs, even at church.

School had started back for Sabrina so she was busy as well. Overall I felt like things were dismantling in my life. Since all this is going on now would be the time for me to make things right with my wife, but even Ray Charles could see that she is tired of my shit and just wants to move on from this marriage. I knew Fatima didn't want to be with me anymore, but she also knows I made it clear that her ass ain't leaving this marriage in a divorce!

I was in my office at work trying to concentrate on work. It was Wednesday, the day I do payroll so I know I had a long day ahead of me. No matter how hard I tried to focus, I just couldn't. In two days I would be meeting who ever that woman was that had called my phone last week telling me that they some news about Karla. I was anxious, yet curious to see who the fuck could it be and how she could help me get that crazy ass bitch out of my life.

My cell phone started ringing and I quickly snatched it up in hopes that it was Fatima only to see that it was Karla calling me again. I sent her ass to the voicemail and cut my phone on silent. You would think that a person would just give up and stop calling someone after their calls and texts go unanswered, but not her. Whoever it was that I was meeting this Friday, I really hope they would have the answers to my problems with Karla.

I picked my phone back up and decided to text Fatima and see if she would like to have dinner since I knew she was off tonight.

Me: hey baby I hope your day is going well I was wondering if you would like to have dinner tonight.

Soon as I hit the send button I became nervous as if I was in high school asking my crush out on a date. I sat there looking at my phone anticipating a quick response, but after about five minutes I still haven't received a response. *Maybe she's asleep* I thought to myself. Somehow I felt like the tables have turned in my marriage. Fatima use to be the one with the calling, texting and worried about my well-being and now I find myself doing it! Fuck this! I grabbed my things and the rest of the invoices I had to do for payroll and left for the day.

I was on my way home and this time for Fatima's sake she better be sleep which is why she hasn't still responded to my messages. I pulled up in my driveway and saw that her car was there. I went inside to find it quiet. I went up the stairs into our bedroom where I heard the shower running letting me know she was in the bathroom.

I put my things down on the dresser and went to undress so I could join her in the shower when I heard her phone vibrating on her side of the nightstand. Now normally,

Fatima's phone could be right by me and I wouldn't touch it, hell I never had a reason to. Seeing how things were between us and the way she's been acting lately, I was curious to see who she was talking to. I went over to the night stand and picked up her phone and saw that it didn't have a lock code on it.

I swiped the screen where it opened up directly to her messages and saw that someone with the initial Q was in her messages. I looked through the thread of messages between them both and immediately saw red! From the looks of it, this Q muthafucka was a dude and Fatima's sneaky ass has been talking to him for quite some time.

I threw her phone hard against the wall breaking it and barged into the bathroom. I snatched the shower door open and grabbed her by her hair snatching her ass out.

"You sneaky ass bitch!" I yelled as I dragged her out of the bathroom and into the bedroom throwing her on the bed.

"Oh my God Travis what are you doing?" Fatima screamed as she tried to scramble up away from me on the bed.

I grabbed her by her ankles and slid her back down to me and slapped her so hard in her face that her nose started to bleed. I grabbed both of her hands and pinned them above her head.

"You think I wasn't gone find out about you fucking around with another nigga! That's why yo ass walking around here like I don't fucking exist!" I screamed in her face with spit flying out my mouth.

I was like a raging bull right now on the attack!

"Travis I don't know what you're talking, please get off of me!" Fatima pleaded crying.

Her tears didn't mean shit to me, especially since I know she's lying!

"I swear if you lie to me one more time I'll break your fucking neck! Bitch I saw the messages in your phone! Since you wanna be out here and be sneaky and lie to my face, I'll a make sure yo ass will never do that shit again!"

I still held her arms tight over her head with my right hand and took my free hand to massage my dick. Fatima was already naked from being in the shower before and I had taken off my clothes prior as well.

"Travis please don't do this" she pleaded, but that shit fell on deaf ears.

My dick got hard and I plunged it right into her.

"Ugh" Fatima yelled out in pain.

"Shut the fuck up!" I yelled again in her face.

I bit down on her neck viciously as I kept plunging

hard in and out of her. She wasn't wet but that didn't stop me. I felt pleasure and power. I continued to fuck Fatima hard as her cries became louder and louder. Hearing how she was at my mercy, turned me on even more.

"Ah!" I screamed out as I came deep inside her.

That was the biggest nut I busted in a long time and I hate that it had come under these circumstances, but I needed to teach Fatima a lesson.

"Now hear me when I say this one last time because I won't say it again! Yo ass ain't getting no divorce and you damn sho' better stop talking to that nigga! If I find out you on some sneaky shit again Fatima I swear next time will be far worse!" I threatened as I stared in her eyes letting her know not to fuck with me.

She just stared back at me crying and shaking with nothing but fear in her eyes. I finally got up from on top of her and went into the bathroom to clean myself up. This shit was far from over with her ass because now I was determined to find out who the fuck this Q nigga was!

KARLA

Paul's ass was back to ignoring me and I was sick of it! I knew I was wrong the last time we met up by blackmailing him into fucking me, but he left me no choice just like he's doing now. The last time we were together I could tell that he didn't want to be there. He wasn't his usual passionate self and fucked me as if I was a hoe on the street.

I thought by me taking it any way he was giving it to me would make him soften up a bit, but it didn't. Even at church he avoided me by leaving as soon as service was over and not greeting us on his way out. I haven't been seeing Fatima at church lately either. I don't know what was going on, but Travis' ass was really starting to get on my damn nerves!

What he didn't know though, was that the last time we were together I placed an app on his phone that allowed me to know his whereabouts from my phone. I did that before with Paul in the beginning of our marriage, but I got tired of catching him with different whores every damn week and beating their asses so I decided to just disable it. I know I shouldn't be worried this much about another woman's husband, especially when I have a husband of my own; but I love Travis.

After trying to call him again and getting his voicemail, I decided that enough was enough. I opened up my app and punched in his number. After a couple of minutes I got a ping notification of his destination. From the address it gave me, I knew he wasn't home. I jumped and threw on some jeans, t-shirt and a pair of my Nikes and hauled ass downstairs to my car.

Paul was at the church handling some business, at least that's what he told me so I didn't have to worry about explaining to him where I was going. I punched the address into my GPS and headed into its direction. I was driving for about a good thirty minutes before I approached my exit. I turned off the highway where the GPS led me to a fucking motel!

I fucking knew it! I said out loud as I headed into the parking lot. This muthafucka had a nerve to be fucking me and another bitch! I circled the parking lot until I spotted his car and parked across from it. I wish I could go inside and ask what room his ass was in, but I didn't want to take the risk of somebody recognizing me so I just cut my car off and waited.

After about two hours, I heard the chirping of his car alarm and saw the lights flashing. I saw him and another figure walking towards his car. I jumped out of my car and ran up behind him.

"So this what we doing now Travis!" I yelled as I hit him on the back hard.

"What the fuck!" he yelled out as he turned around.

Right when Travis turned around, so did the person he was with. I stepped back and couldn't believe this shit!" Tonya?"

TO BE CONTINUED

CPSIA information can be obtained
at www.ICGtesting.com
Printed in the USA
LVOW03s0846040218
565241LV00001B/204/P